Alan Sillitoe  ourteen
to work in va.. traffic
control assistant .... luction
in 1945.

He enlisted in R..d spent
two years on active service in Malaya as a wireless operator.
At the end of 1949 he was invalided out of the service with
a hundred per cent disability pension.

He began writing, and lived for six years in France and
Spain. His first stories were published in the *Nottinghamshire
Weekly Guardian*. In 1958 *Saturday Night and Sunday Morning*
was published, and *The Loneliness of the Long-distance Runner*,
which won the Hawthornden Prize for literature, came out
the following year. Both these books were made into films.

Further works include *Key to the Door*, *The Ragman's
Daughter* and *The General* (both also filmed), *The William
Posters Trilogy*, *A Start in Life*, *Raw Material*, *The Widower's
Son*, *The Second Chance* – as well as six volumes of poetry.
His latest books are *Her Victory*, *The Lost Flying Boat* and
Down from the Hill. With his wife, Ruth Fainlight, he divides
his time between London and a house in Kent.

By the same author

Fiction

Saturday Night and Sunday Morning
The Loneliness of the Long-distance Runner
Key to the Door
The Ragman's Daughter
The Death of William Posters
A Tree on Fire
Guzman, Go Home
A Start in Life
Travels in Nihilon
Raw Material
Men, Women and Children
The Flame of Life
The Widower's Son
The Storyteller
The Second Chance
Her Victory
The Lost Flying Boat
Down from the Hill

Poetry

The Rats and Other Poems
A Falling out of Love and Other Poems
Love in the Environs of Voronezh
Storm and Other Poems
Snow on the North Side of Lucifer
Sun Before Departure

Plays

All Citizens Are Soldiers (with Ruth Fainlight)
Three Plays

Non-fiction

Road to Volgograd

Essays

Mountains and Caverns

For children

The City Adventures of Marmalade Jim
Big John and the Stars
The Incredible Fencing Fleas
Marmalade Jim on the Farm
Marmalade Jim and the Fox

ALAN SILLITOE

The General

GRAFTON BOOKS

A Division of the Collins Publishing Group

LONDON GLASGOW
TORONTO SYDNEY AUCKLAND

Grafton Books
A Division of the Collins Publishing Group
8 Grafton Street, London W1X 3LA

Published by Grafton Books 1986

First published in Great Britain by
W. H. Allen & Co. Ltd. 1960

ISBN 0-586-06571-7

Printed and bound in Great Britain by
Collins, Glasgow

Set in Baskerville

NOTE: East and West in this novel bear no relation to the east and west of modern times.

1

The train was carried slowly through the night on rhythmi-
cally beating pistons, its centipede-brown belly sending the
same morse-code symbol for hour after hour into black
woods or arable rolling plain. Its sound occasionally varied
on the final click: der-der-der-dun, der-der-der-dun, der-
der-der-dack, der-der-der-dun. A lighter rattle under the
wheels was a bridge being crossed, and out of the window
a broad river curled away under the moon. When the
singing of its wheels became heavy and even, the train was
still in the forest, and orange sparks rising from its chimney
resembled flakes of sawdust, giving it the appearance of a
minuscular saw driving a vein through the earth's darkness.

Evart reached for the flask of cold coffee wedged in the
bend of the wooden seat, unscrewed the cup, and poured
himself a drink. They had been two days in the train, and
no one knew to what town or city it was going, each
passenger perceiving only that, on waking up each morning, the engine was touched by warm autumnal rays of the
rising sun.

Holding the emptied cup – whose contents had in no
way helped to clear the fatigue and travel-dust in his throat
– he ruminatively traced the journey they had made thus
far. The northern seaport had been so crowded with ships
that they had formed a living suburban growth attached to
the city itself, planned in complicated laneways on the
water. An unassuming air of chaos brooded over the port,
and to transfer men and luggage to shore had taken several
hours.

A waiting train took them four hundred miles into a
countryside dreary and desolate; then between ranges of

low-spurred and forest-patched hills that exhibited black scabs of village settlements not yet returned to life; across green-sedge marshes with vague shapes of blue water extending distantly westwards; finally traversing a region of rich well-tilled soil upon which life seemed more normal.

In thirty hours the capital was reached, a million houses whose outskirts resembled a band of black ribbon, having been blasted and strangled in the quick siege before its capture. They moved westwards from there on newly repaired lines, and were disturbed many times in the night as the train shunted through sidings, coupled and uncoupled, stopped and started for no apparent reason. Stations came closer together, and furnaces glowed green and orange against the sky. During their slow progress through the industrial region Evart remembered his geography books, faint school memories of dull facts hammered home by teachers who culled them from books whose authors had paraphrased them from other books: an unknown quantity of vast wheatlands mechanically farmed, hundred thousand cities black with collective tractor industries. Whole regions, marked by mineral riverbends or geologically rich ranges, were set beyond the farthest pampered soils of Europe, outcropped provinces chimney-stacked from end to end, a black conveyor belt of power, one of dozens that had to be defeated not because two similar parts of the world entertained parallel ideas of grandeur, but because each insisted on using different methods to get there.

Leaning his sallow face against the cool glass of the carriage window he saw a soft pink light towards the west. A red sky every morning for a thousand years would not be enough, he thought, to account for this war. The plain seemed endless: clumps of trees transfixed by the dawn's bayonets, empty defendable gullies, running away from the track, a few clouds reconnoitring to the north, not heeding the train that threaded itself through the eyes of derelict

8

stations. On the platform of one stood a half asleep soldier on guard, whose greatcoat, fastened at the waist by a piece of rope, was so ragged it looked as though he were wearing it inside out. He lifted a hand to his face and yawned as the train passed him. Village buildings straggled nearby: impossible to know where they were because all nameplates had been taken away, and the trainwheels rumbled on as through a discharted land.

He had been by the window since four o'clock and, turning back to the carriage, he lit a cigarette with the stub of one just finished. The train's night trek had shaken him from one harrowing dream to another, and he had hardly slept. Certain of his dreams entailed hard mental work, the solving of simple conundrums whose arithmetical answers, common knowledge in daylight, had not only eluded him but became monstrous figures of frustration. He frequently regained consciousness from these struggles having lost all sense of time and place, doubting the reality of their journey. For a while he could neither think of the date nor season, and only knew the hour of day with any accuracy when dawn or dusk broke up the shadows in the carriage: the watch on his wrist ticked when he held it up to his ear, but its automatic measuring no longer meant anything.

Dim blue bulbs along the ceiling suddenly went out, taking their faint, half dead shadows with them. Most of the players, not yet knowing that it was dawn, still slept, sprawling over wooden seats, leaning on each other or on their instruments, grunting and moving with each jolt of the crawling train. Two violinists quarrelled with unusual bitterness over a packet of coffee, and Evart listened as if they were discussing some interesting philosophical problem.

'I bought it last night at a station, from the old woman who guarded her stock with the big dogs. It cost a good deal of my allowance, so I'm not going to give it away or let you steal it.' He held out his hands, as if the matter was

9

now settled and the other man would give the coffee back without a word.

Dawn was a bad time for agreement: 'And if you remember I gave you half the money towards it, so it's as much mine as yours.'

'That doesn't mean you can take all of it.' He was almost weeping with vexation, and Evart looked away, filled with a blind wish that they would solve their difference quickly. Beyond the window, on and below the horizontal line, explosions were bursting in cups of steel light. Flames twinkled. Some resembled tiny flowers; others lifted and died in half a second like the fitful stirring of drunken and bloodshot eyes. The carriage gangway was blocked in places with stacked instrument boxes, and string net racks above bulged with personal luggage. Most of the windows were closed tight against the cold night air, and a stale smell of sleep lingered.

The bickering violinists became unimportant, were swamped by others moving, by the sound of their resentment at being pulled out of a sleep that, however disturbed and light, was better than living with the continual question that filled their minds during daytime. Armgardson led a party towards the guard's van in search of hot water for tea and coffee, and two flautists by the far door were sharing a mirror, telling each other how badly they needed a shave, trying to wield a razor against the sway of the train.

They made a slow semicircle around a burned-down village, and the roaring of lorries came from a motordump in its ruined centre. A line of dishevelled soldiers were passing petrol tins to each other, and several vehicles were leaving the ruins, strung out in a line on their way to the east. Evart resented the fact that they were not travelling in the same direction as the train, feeling as if an outrageous act of betrayal – that he could do nothing to stop – were going on before his eyes. He looked away, seeing the train's black engine on the broadgauge line, straightening out from a wide curve by the village. A range of low hills lay before them, and a weak sun shone through strato-cumulus cloud, illuminating spurs and folds and clumps of trees on higher hills beyond, from which numerous puffs of smoke arose, as if they were approaching a convention of Red Indian signallers. The visible world of battle through the window no longer seemed so remote, and the silent film he saw began to assume a particular soundtrack that made him feel sick at the stomach. He thought soberly of all the 'Petitions of Objection' filed against the War Ministry's decision to send the orchestra to the front and entertain the Army, smiling ironically at his belated discovery that in war there is no such thing as objection.

'It's no use brooding on it,' someone said to him.

Smiling at such an apt early-morning remark Evart turned from the window, as Starnberg sat down on the opposite seat. 'War's the only time you can't profit from experience,' Starnberg went on, crossing one fat leg over the other. 'In war you do one foolish thing after another, but have to keep on doing them either because you're ordered to do so, or are placed in a position by idiots where you can't do anything else.'

Evart nodded towards explosions in the distance that Starnberg could not see. 'Beyond that,' he said in a jerky irritated voice, 'you have to do what you're told, in peace or war. So we're led to believe.'

'Do you think it's true then?' Starnberg asked, as if to say that Evart would be foolish if he did. 'Do you really believe it's worse there than it is here? Whenever you get a line of battle dividing two countries the same laws reign in both, you can be sure of that. We didn't ask to come to the front, we were ordered to do so, and you can't deny it.' After these heated statements he glanced out of the window.

Evart raised his voice also, more than was necessary to

11

be heard above the noise of the train. 'No one is so stupid any more as to believe anything a government says. That's true. But do you think it stops us doing what they tell us? We're going to discover what it'll be like to play the Fifth in some troops' mess hall under fire, and I for one would rather sit at home in my flat and have it described to me by a war correspondent, or read about it in some book, than have to find out for myself. But we have to do what we're told,' he ended resignedly.

'So much for my wisdom,' Starnberg said, leaning back on the wooden seat and laughing, wrinkling his eyes so that they were nearly closed.

'What else can you do but laugh if you're to survive?' Evart said, his voice indicating both cynicism and admiration. 'You're quite right. This is the biggest joke I've heard of, the Government sending a symphony orchestra to entertain the troops, ninety per cent of whom have never heard a symphony in their lives and don't want to hear one. I pity them, in fact, having to sit through a concert. And here we are, too close to the front for comfort, part of some propaganda scheme of the Ministry of Information to let the enemy know it's a cultured army they're fighting. As if it makes any difference. As if anyone will ever know. It makes me sick, I tell you.' A brief, outmoded, strong voice spouting of leadership and responsibility came up in him: You shouldn't say such things, not even to Starnberg. You're in charge of this orchestra, and you've got to keep it going, no matter what they have to face. But he crushed the voice, that was unremembered as soon as it had disappeared.

'Cynicism, amusement and resignation,' Starnberg said, 'is the best attitude for survival. For instance, we've only signed a contract for six weeks at the front and then it'll be finished: we'll be going back east and looking forward to reasonable comfort again.' His gaiety left him when he realized aloud: 'But they can always extend our contract. Of course they can. They don't have to consult us.'

'The comfort of a civilization at war,' Evart mocked, staring doggedly at the green bare hills. The carriage was hot and stuffy with cigarette smoke, though every window had been opened in the hope of catching some movement of air from the train's slow speed. He found that these arguments had no neat and logical end; they became bogged in a swamp of personal rage, with both of them arguing vehemently against the same thing, yet strangely turned in at one another. Starnberg seemed to realize this also: he shrugged his shoulders and walked away, a short fat figure spanning heaps of boxes in the gangway.

There was some activity now on the hill slopes. War had robbed the turf of all distinguishing marks of season; the soil was untilled and colourless, an upturned desert where soldiers were building ramparts and digging trenches, and teams of mules hauling long-barrelled guns into place. Bayonets flashed in the sun like heliographs, and troops, from their grime and fatigue, smiled and waved at the passing train. He felt someone beside him, and Bender the 'cellist stood with a hand resting on the seat's curved top to brace himself against the shaking. 'Our soldiers seem to be busy over there. We must be quite near the front line.'

Evart saw anxiety in his intense, heavily browed eyes: they took in what was happening beyond the window as a composite yet clear picture but, as opposed to the flashing bayonets, they could rip little distance into any meaningful future. He had noticed before how deceptive were such eyes; what you hoped was insight would invariably turn out to be an unpredictable world-weariness.

'I expect we'll be leaving the train some time today,' Bender said quickly. 'It needs quite a lot of endurance to stay on a train for so long. Some of our men think we're getting close to the front.'

'We're probably a long way from it,' Evart told him. If I

sound too reassuring he won't believe me, he added to himself, watching the timid 'cellist step to the end of the carriage and push open the lavatory door.

Those who had finished washing hung towels from the racks, or trapped them firmly in the windows so that they flapped outside like signals of surrender. Evart pulled down his leather suitcase and clicked it open, studying the civilized arrangement of shirts, brushes, ties – a small perishable appendage to a meticulous mind – before taking out what he needed. Starnberg, wearing heavy spectacles, waved an unfolded map before him. 'I found this under one of the seats. It's fifty years old,' he said eagerly when Evart leaned over to look, 'and very interesting.' He sat down heavily and spread it across his knees, his finger pointing among diverse colours that were faded with age. 'Look, here's this range of mountains. According to the newspapers we should be right at the front by now.'

'According to those gun flashes as well,' Evart said wryly.

Starnberg's face was worried as he examined the map, then he looked up and smiled. 'Maps fascinate me. When I was a boy I wanted to be a surveyor, or a general, anything that was connected with maps. But surveying meant too much discomfort, and soldiering too much danger, so I studied music.' Evart laughed with him, and Starnberg was showing his map to someone else.

It would have made a superb view in other circumstances. The height of the hills diminished towards a flattened expanse of green pasture-land, dotted sparsely with settlements, darkened here and there by patches of forest with such indistinct edges that they were taken at first sight for tremendous cloud shadows fallen to earth. A string of small pools by a river to the north shone like silver coins. Cottonlike gunpuffs and fireflashes had a ribbon of road connecting two villages, and between the foothills and

14

another settlement a road was blocked by lorries, tanks, guns and soldiers. The train jolted around a bend and threw those standing against the wooden seats, and Evart's shaving-box fell to the floor. Passing another village he counted thirty heavy tanks assembled nearby, and saw on the higher crests entrenchments of mass artillery. Soldiers in the fields were digging small pits and cutting down trees for cover. Thinking back on this time, he asked himself what had been in his mind, and the only answer he could provide was: hardly anything, indifference, a numbness from too much travel and too little sleep. It never even occurred to him that there might be something he could do, or should do, or that it was even necessary to do anything at all. And in any case it would have made no difference, he told himself.

Walking unsteadily up the gangway he pushed open the lavatory door. It was empty, the only place on the train that gave a promise of peace. He slipped the catch and took off his coat. His dark eyes rimless with sleep, and thick half grey hair were reflected in the stained mirror – salient features keeping at bay those subtleties of expression that sometimes reveal the deeper truths of a face to the eyes of a woman, a brother, or a comrade, though rarely to the beholder of the face itself. Water came from the taps, swirling warm around his dipped fingers, and he wedged himself into a narrow space between two walls to keep his body still. He pulled the razor lightly over the white foam, up and down, leaving a clean lane of pink flesh. The train entered a tunnel and because the light that went on was too dim to see by he waited until it emerged from the cutting. The battle had receded, or the train had veered away from it. He whistled to himself in a sudden burst of freedom, feeling as though a load of irritating responsibility that had sat on his shoulders for as long as he could remember had for some reason been taken away. The train, even in its swaying, became his companion: it was carrying him somewhere, to places on the map that he had not visited before, and taking him away, on the music of its wheels, from places he had stayed in too long. His face being tolerably smooth, he bent his shoulders over the basin to swill off the soap.

'Evart! Evart!'

He hurriedly packed his things and pulled the door open: 'What is it?' he asked brusquely.

Starnberg stepped out of the way to let him pass. 'We're getting near the front,' he called from behind.

Evart laughed: 'Of course we are. It's a good sign. We'll be at wherever it is soon. Then perhaps we'll be given a proper meal.' He walked along the gangway to his seat. His mind tried to join the past with now, to pin the two points together with the sharp dividers of memory – otherwise the sweet earth bearing the people he had said goodbyes to would become too much like a dream; a state which frightened him more than whatever catastrophe the orchestra might run into on its mad train journey, because he had never been the sort of person who remembered dreams. But in trying to reach the immediate past he had merely frog-landed into a limbo of petty psychologizing – a state he loathed. So rather than stay in it he drew his sense back to the present, glad of it as a foolproof anchor despite the fact that he was in a train and heading for God knew where.

Starnberg was still with him when he looked up from packing his things back in the case. 'Don't you think we're too near the front line, Evart?'

'We've been too close to it for the last few days,' he said amicably, looking out of the window. The track ran by a straight flat road, and slightly wounded soldiers were trudging back to the safety of the hills. They shouted and gesticulated, but the orchestra heard no words uttered above the confusion growing around them. 'They're telling us to get out,' someone shouted.

16

Evart turned angrily: 'No, they aren't. If anyone jumps they'll be killed.'

The train went slower, and everybody thought with relief that it was going to stop, but at the next station it leapt forward and travelled much faster than before. Lorries and ambulances moved at slow speed along the road in the opposite direction. Shellbursts were heard above the rumble of the train, and the sky in front was covered by a haze of smoke through which the weak, pale eye of the sun came now and again. Several houses in the village were burning; others were heaps of brick straggled by twisted telephone wires. The sensation that controlled Evart's mind was one of curiosity. He stood up to look at the wrecked village, holding himself steady by gripping an overhead rack as the train rocked beneath his feet. Now on the descending gradient it curved into the high walls of a cutting, traversing a ledge that gave another view of the wide plain in front, with the noise of artillery following it through each concealed part of the track. Warm sun spread over the windows as they came out of a tunnel. Someone tapped him on the shoulder. 'What is it?' he asked, turning round. 'Oh, it's you, Viccadi.'

In the questioning, middle-aged eyes he saw a frightened animal demand that he pacify them, strengthen them, lift them to a higher plane of courage that they were not capable of attaining. But he had not the hypnotic force to help anyone or even himself to reach this state. He felt fatalistic, therefore calm, but such hard and insecure tranquillity could not be disseminated to other hearts beyond his own. He pulled his fingers tightly over the flesh on his neck until he felt pain. No one could yet tell what was happening. A 'cellist behind Viccadi cried with false enthusiasm: 'I suppose we'll be getting out of here soon?'

'I'll want a long rest,' someone shouted from down the carriage, 'when we do get out.'

17

'There'll be no long rest for us,' the drummer called. 'We'll be playing Schumann tonight, you see.'

Armgardson stepped from the open door near the lavatory: 'By the sound of those guns we'll be playing to the devil,' he shouted.

Viccadi, looking at Evart, demanded: 'Aren't we in danger from the guns yet?'

'I don't think so. And if we are, we'll have to get used to it. We'll be hearing them a lot in the next few weeks.'

A man who had overheard said truculently: 'If I hear too much of them you'll find me making my own way home.'

Evart's reply to this was drowned by a more emphatic voice: 'This train had better stop soon or you'll see me getting off and going back now. We aren't going too fast to jump out.'

Soldiers were streaming towards the burning village, as if its beacon-signal was a rendezvous for safety. Many had been killed by the bombardment and lay twisted on the ground, looking like bundles of deserted clothing scattered between trees and by the roadside. Evart saw some of them move: They lay in blue and crimson pools, symbols of a pain whose intensity he could not imagine; and because they weren't dead and set beyond the enduring of it he felt ashamed and resentful against them.

The train, running into a tunnelled arch of gunfire, swayed as though it would dance off the rails. Several voices began shouting at once, most of them asking Evart questions that he could not answer. A jolt of the train shook loose a tuft of hair and he brushed it back with a quick movement. He was convinced that there was nothing to be done, his mind on this fact having been made up for years: his personality was so formed that at a moment like this there would be nothing he could do; and nothing, no inspired act would come to make him do something. It was the reverse of panic that gripped him, and just as lethal.

They were in a train: they could only get out when it drew in to a station. And in any case, was there really any danger? The train would stop in a few minutes, and they would be taken by lorry to a quiet area. What was the use of shouting? A few of the players were taking down towels and packing their cases, while others could not resist looking out of the windows.

'I don't know what's going on,' Evart said to those clamouring around him. 'It'll be all right if you sit down and keep calm.' Someone laughed, pointing to clouds of gunsmoke too close to the train. 'Keep calm,' he shouted. 'There's nothing to worry about.'

They were passing through a recent battleground. Gun-pits were smashed and abandoned. Crippled tanks lay silent and still; some were shrouded in fresh plumes of smoke and flame; others, still intact, were beleaguered within pools of quietly burning oil. Brown lips of rocky earth had been thrown up from the fields, and it seemed only a matter of time before the train was derailed by a crater, or toppled from a collapsing bridge into a river.

'What do you think has happened?' Starnberg asked.

Evart's face was pale. 'How do I know?' he snapped. 'God knows. It seems we've run into an attack. I don't know.'

The speed of the train was slow but consistent, and it seemed as if they would travel at that speed for ever, no matter what lay in its way. The hills were left behind, and straight level track ran towards a large area of open country. The carriage was filled with shouts of anger and alarm. 'Where are we going?' Bender the 'cellist demanded of Evart. 'What's wrong with the driver? Why doesn't he stop the train?'

'He's a spy, that's why. He's on their side. Can't somebody do something?'

Evart saw a white frightened face through the crowd; a

19

more belligerent figure hid it from view. 'I'm getting out of this,' it cried.

'Too far,' someone else shouted. 'It's too far, too close to the front line. The contract didn't say we should go this far.' Starnberg's heavy unshaven face was yellow, his lips trembling. 'What can we do?' he asked. 'Can't we do something?'

'I don't know what we can damned well do,' Evart cried. His tone changed: 'We don't know whether there's any reason to be alarmed yet.' He had been shocked at the heightened sound of his voice, yet justified it by telling himself how tired he was of people asking questions when they already knew the answers as well as he did. They only ask, he thought angrily, like children, because they want reassuring with lies. An irate violinist pushed his way to the door, unlocked it, and flung it open so that it swung backwards and forwards against the side of the coach.

'He's going to jump! Hold him!'

Evart ran: too late. The man had already leapt on to the road. He stumbled, lay still for a moment, then stood up dizzily, and before he was cut from view by a turn of the train they saw him walking towards the ruined village in the midst of a straggle of unarmed soldiers.

Smoke and oil fumes, caught by the train's movement, came into the carriage. Evart, trying to close the door, was dragged clear from behind, and two more men dropped from the train. They lay stunned on the road, then were out of sight. Others tried to force their way through, but Starnberg pushed them away. Evart closed the door and returned to his seat, determined not to stop anyone else from leaving. No one wanted to try, however, and he stared out of the window, weary and tired, hoping for a quick end to the journey. He felt himself dreaming, falling asleep from the gentle persistent rocking of the train. The slow thud of bursting small-calibre shells was varied by the sound of rifles and machine guns. With half closed eyes he heard Starnberg arguing at the door against someone who could not make up his mind whether or not to jump out of the train. He opened his eyes and saw three shells form a triangular explosion within a few yards of each other, like old friends accidentally meeting, maddened by the joys of life. Smoke and earth mixed with pyrotechnic fervour, threw out two protective arms, burst asunder, subsided.

'Can you see them?' a voice cried. 'They're not ours.'

Uniformed men were running forward in groups, stumbling over stony uneven ground. 'Where are they? Where?'

'Are you blind? Over there. See them?'

'Of course they're ours. You're all frightened when there's no need to be.' Everyone suddenly stopped talking, as if to conserve their nervous energy while waiting for a quick end to this uncertain theatrical performance. It took too much strength to speak now. It was better to wait and see, and spend yourself afterwards. The pale mauve sky, warm with dust and smoke and half sun, was sliced from Evart's vision by a shallow cutting on whose banks yellow and pink flowers grew from obdurate soil, and when the steep sides fell away he saw the northern part of the plain now scattered with blazing fires.

'We're in the middle of a bloody battle,' someone shouted.

'Don't jump,' Starnberg commanded. 'You'll be killed. It's too late.'

Evart looked along the line. No one leapt from the train. Windows were closed tight, as if glass would protect them from stray bullets, and the air in the carriage was thick and hot. A group of horsemen with automatic weapons slung across their shoulders turned from a field to look at the train as it veered in their direction. Starnberg left his position as watchdog by the door and walked carefully up the gangway. 'Let them jump if they like,' he said to Evart. 'We're in trouble, and if they care to risk their necks trying to get out of it I'm not going to stop them.' Evart saw his harassed perspiring face, collar loosened at the neck, and shaking hands that he steadied by gripping the seat-top as soon as Evart noticed them. 'I've never been in a situation like this,' he suddenly said, 'when there's absolutely nothing to be done.'

A horseman advanced towards the train and, after waiting calmly where the track curved, galloped alongside it for several minutes, and performed an acrobatic feat by throwing himself into the engine cab. He pointed his rifle at the bewildered drivers. 'I certainly don't know what all this means,' Starnberg was saying.

Evart pushed by him, and ran along the carriage shouting: 'Hold yourselves firm. The train's going to stop.'

Most of them heard, realized what he meant, wedged arms and legs and shoulders tight, a pressure saving them from being jolted on to packages in the gangway. Cases slid from the rack, clattered against seats, brought cries from those on whom they fell. The hard shoulder of an uncontrolled body was flung at Evart, throwing him back against the wood. Unlatched doors swung and hammered freely; those who had not secured a good hold were knocked down. Several who had been winded by blows in the stomach lay with grey and petrified faces, unable to move, as if held against the floor by an invisible boot.

With arms relaxed, they recovered dizzily, rubbing bruises and reviling those responsible for pulling-up on such a short stretch of track. They looked at each other, unable to believe in the silence now that the train had stopped: the noise of rolling wheels with which they had lived for the past four days had been like an unseen friend, and the stillness left by its strange absence seemed uncanny, a stab-in-the-back remoteness that took their courage away. Someone began to weep.

'You shouted out just in time,' Starnberg said, smiling at returning sounds of doors closing, cases being clicked shut, the walk of footsteps.

'We'll be taken prisoner,' Evart said, a fact which, though generally realized, brought consternation to many faces. He was glad not to be afraid himself and, followed by Starnberg, pushed his way through a crowd near the door. 'Let me open it,' he demanded sharply, 'then we can get out.'

'Don't go,' someone cried behind, pulling him back. 'Get down. Their tanks are coming!' Evart pushed the hand away, peered outside, tried to drag secrets from the thickening smoke. A single tank nosed its way through, grey, ponderous, cautious. Behind it a dozen spears of white flame suddenly shot skywards with a terrible heart-rending roar that jarred and rattled through the whole train. The orchestra within drew back as if the invisible power that had pushed itself against the windows would break through with the next explosion and scorch them to death. An uneven line of tanks now came out of the smoke, rolling over open ground on both sides of the halted train. They emitted another salvo from their guns, and went on to the foothills of the nearby mountains. Soldiers followed, with fixed bayonets whose steel was caught by sunlight that came through a gap in the smoke. No one could speak above the roar of tank engines, and they stood by doors and windows watching the advance sweep by. Evart felt afraid for the first time. A few miles away a tank was suddenly covered by a loop of flame; it glowed white and brilliant for a second, then spouted into the air as if melted by the heat; a further explosion hid it in a hillock of dust and vapour.

More groups of soldiers came through the smoke. One company detached itself and clamoured along the train, placing hands on the window glass, touching the huge wheels, and trying to turn door handles. The horseman who had stopped the train returned to his patrol. His friends had waited for him, and were now laughing at his exploit, pointing at the monster he had miraculously defeated. Suddenly they urged their horses forward and galloped off towards the hills, following the track of the armour.

Evart flung open the carriage door. The air was clearing; smoke, after the passing of the tanks, was drifting away. With silence in the carriage behind, he looked out at the soldiers standing along the train. He had seen photographs of them before, no worse than any other soldiers, capable of kindness no doubt to each other. But this was war and they were enemies, and to slay, pillage and torture was second nature to them, a sublime perquisite of their expended energy and peril. How else could it be? he asked himself. Culled from the cities and farms of their endless continent they were drilled into unthinking horde-formation and sent teeming against the trenches and defence-lines which they attacked with the fearlessness of twilight intelligence. Thin, hardy, raw-boned, they were death's harvest, a quota that death must have, serving a double purpose of defending a nation so that others could be born in safety, and at the same time making way for those that were born, providers and protectors of living space by their own disappearance. They were lightly armed, scantily dressed, living for the most part on conquered or recaptured land, where a field of green shoots would support a battalion as it passed like locusts, or a bombed-out village give it shelter for the winter. They were a monsoon of armies in a world climatically perilous for men, advancing and retreating, planned offensive and unplanned withdrawal, taking a high rainfall of blood over unirrigated land.

The battle had rolled by, with gunfire no more than a tremor to the east. Evart's watch told him it was ten o'clock. Clouds of smoke and dust drifted from the hills, and the yellow blurred sun was high enough to give off an intense heat. He thought it strange that the battle should already be over, for the end of a battle meant that you were free from death, while it seemed to him that death

24

was about to begin for himself and his orchestra. Those soldiers nearest the train pressed forward and unlooped their automatic rifles, pointing them at the window. Forest depths were reflected in their blue-grey eyes, eyes that for most of their lives had recorded nothing but vast and vacant spaces: plains, immense ranges of blue mountains, wide-sweeping empty rivers, landscapes with soft colours of blue and yellow, yet landscapes poisonous like certain flowers with similar colours and tints: country from which life had to be stalked, clawed, stabbed, taken by force and spiteful barbarity. Their Gorshek eyes were marked with all this, eyes that gave the impression of peace and gentleness, but eyes that had drawn a living from the sort of landscape imprinted in them, and were therefore alien to peace and gentleness.

2

Evart descended from the carriage, calling out that the orchestra begin unloading the instruments and luggage, and stack them on the ground. He walked along the track, exhorted them to move quickly, the soldiers stepping out of his way to let him go by. Starnberg lowered himself awkwardly: 'The instruments will be no use to us,' he exclaimed, his voice pulling Evart from his achievement, making him once more aware of the danger he was in.

'It'll give us something to do,' he told him curtly, afraid that his risk should be set at nothing by Starnberg's futile remark. He threw off his coat in the heat, and the movement of unloading took everyone from their state of petrified fear. 'Keep working,' he said in a loud voice. 'Let them have something to stare at.'

As more members of the orchestra came from the train the Gorshek soldiers withdrew pace by pace and gave them room. For a mob they were unusually quiet, curious perhaps, and apart from an occasional voice remarking on what was seen at the end of a pointed finger, the only sound was the rattle and click of rifles seeking different positions so that arms could relax or rest. Evart lifted one case on to another and, straightening himself, looked at the speculating line of soldiers to see what change was in their mood. None. He turned to go on working. It may be, he thought, surprised at his sudden hope, that the look and smell of what seem our riches remind them too vividly of their own officers and the distance that separates them. Yet the feeling of death in the middle of his coatless and exposed back would not leave him.

'All we need is time,' he said to Starnberg. 'If we can

26

stop them sensing any fear they might not think it so natural to kill us.'

'Judging by the look of them it'll be a difficult policy to carry out,' Starnberg grumbled. 'Though I suppose it's better to work.'

Evart wondered what would happen if they ceased their activity, but crushed the thought before it gained control.

'No,' he said loudly to someone nearby, 'you can't stack such big boxes on the instruments' – and took over the man's work, glad to feel his hands warming to the weight of heavy cases as he pulled them out of the way. The soldiers speculated more noisily, a development that produced in Evart a fear deeper than that of death: he stood before enemies that were greater than enemies who could merely kill you: by killing you they destroyed that which you had spent your life trying to represent and propagate. Thus he realized fully for the first time the greater meaning of death. He was encircled by a force that he had feared all his life, but one that had so far existed only in his imagination and occasional nightmares: an illiterate mass suddenly able to destroy something they could never comprehend. They would annihilate the orchestra for no reason, on an impulse, like a bored child killing ants for fun when he did not realize the meaning of death. Yet to kill for fun was, to them, reason itself. He wanted to tell Starnberg this, but did not think it would do either of them any good to exchange such thoughts.

The carriage was empty and the last instrument and luggage box stacked. Piles of cases formed a frail barrier between orchestra and soldiers, the latter now shouting so loudly that the orchestra had to raise their voices to make themselves heard. It was no longer a question of discussing what they should do; most of them had nothing to say, and the lifting of voices was confined to those who did not yet realize that there was no more to be done. A general outcry ran among them: 'How could such a thing have happened?'

– followed by an impatient and irritated voice that bayed loud above the other noise: 'A stupid mistake has been made by someone.'

A shrill, hysterical cry came into the argument: 'Anything is possible when it's already happened. We want to know what to do now.'

Bender retorted in an uncertain tone: 'But we don't know what it is yet. This might be only what they call an armed reconnaissance, and these soldiers will go back to their lines soon and just leave us here. Then we'll be free again.'

'Let's face it: we've been captured.'

'Wait and see.'

Modified thoughts leapt up to the wave of anger that followed the admission of capture. 'Even if it has happened there'll be a counter-attack and we'll find ourselves safe behind the lines before tonight.'

'We'll probably never live through a counter-attack,' came the quick retort. Another person wanted to know what a counter-attack was, but no one bothered to tell him.

'We certainly won't live through this,' cried a voice next to Evart that was immediately contradicted.

'I doubt whether any of our soldiers will be left to make a counter-attack,' the same voice shouted bravely above the argument. Evart listened for a while, standing silently with folded arms, a cigarette in his mouth. The fleeting fear of death was succeeded by a feeling of hopeless contest: like finally breaking into a telephone circuit and finding that every speaker in a city system is talking at the same time. The odds are too great for hope, he thought; in fact there are no odds at all. These are the animal blind forces about to act. A millionth part of nature's smallest cycle is ready to move, and it will be unnoticed because all those factors that went before and contributed to this infinitesimally small movement also went unnoticed. So why should I

28

care, or try to stop any move? Would all the anguish be worthwhile just to postpone it for what might be a long time to us, but immeasurably small compared to a timeless universe? His line of thought swam into a mist. Looking up, Starnberg was near him.

'What I think is that the government deliberately sent our train through the lines so that we'd be captured. I reason it out like this: if the Gorsheks kill us all, our side will have some nice atrocity propaganda, and if they don't kill us, at least they'll have proof, in the form of a symphony orchestra, that our army is cultured.' Starnberg was pleased with his explanation. 'Don't you agree that I'm right?'

'You have too much imagination,' Evart said ironically. A group of soldiers nearby were arguing among themselves. Several rifleshots cracked like whips into the air, and he wondered where the bullets would fall. Starnberg inclined his pale obese cheek towards the soldiers: 'And they don't have enough imagination, unfortunately.'

Evart told himself that Starnberg was too good-natured to feel insulted. You could disagree with him as much as you liked and he would never retaliate with any strength – and his rationality was defence enough. 'I don't think you care whether or not we are killed,' he said in a level voice, thrusting his hands deeply into jacket pockets.

'Whether I mind or not will make little difference,' Evart said stiffly. He looked across the plain, at darkening humps of smoke drifting away from the hills. They were startled by the train-whistle sounding above the clamour of the soldiers. The carriage rolled along the rails, and those who were leaning against wheels and doors were jolted from their feet. A sound of ironbound, reverberating chainlinks was relayed heavily along the track, and the train shunted away, leaving the orchestra exposed, standing by stacks of luggage as if at a market stall. A continuous roar of traffic filled the air, vehicles now moving in column along the nearby road, instead of advancing in mass through open

29

country as before. The momentum of the Gorshek offensive was slackening.

'I used to think it would be a good world if all this energy spent in war was used for peaceful things,' Starnberg said, 'but the energy necessary to make a happy and prosperous peace is too small. The only reason there'll always be wars is that man has too much energy, not that he has too little intelligence.'

Evart looked at the threatening movements of the Gorsheks on the edge of the crowd. 'I'd rather the train had stayed where it was,' he said without turning around. 'Yes, I agree,' he added. 'You put it succinctly.'

Starnberg laughed nervously and looked in the same direction. 'Danger makes one more perceptive,' he said, 'that's all. It's not permanent. I'd rather be dull and safe.' His knees were shaking and he sat down on a box. Watching Evart tap a stone loose with the toe of his shoe, the undertone of terror became muted. 'But why aren't you afraid?' he asked, his anxiety returning.

'Because I've nothing to be afraid of.'

Starnberg smiled. 'That hides everything, and tells me nothing. A stonewall hint.'

'If you must sharpen your wits, it's because I don't think there's anything left that can make me afraid, not in the way you're thinking of.'

'After what?'

Evart did not answer. He lit another cigarette.

'Would you be afraid if they killed you?'

Smoking gave him great satisfaction, though without a cigarette he was calm; with one, anxious. 'No,' he said simply.

Starnberg waved his arm to where the orchestra stood. 'Would you be afraid if they killed all of us?'

He did not answer. But there was no escaping such a question. 'Of course,' he said after a pause.

Starnberg was reassured. Evart, amused at the too

30

firm handshake, became uneasy when he realized the importance attached to his words. Starnberg pulled out a white folded handkerchief and padded the sweat from his brow. Evart scoffed silently: He thinks it makes me more human. Scuffling came from the edge of the crowd: the Gorsheks were lunging out with riflebutts. 'Give him your watch,' someone cried. The disturbance died down. Evart wondered why they were waiting. Is it still curiosity? We aren't so different from them, after all. He looked anxiously towards the noise, unable to decide whether it would do any good if he went over to it. 'There's nothing I can do,' he said. But when fighting broke out again he walked towards it, followed by Starnberg.

The air was filled with shouts as they were overwhelmed. The Gorsheks swung out their rifles, thrust forward with elbows and fists to get coats and boots from them, struck even when there was no resistance. Evart felt himself pulled from behind; thin sticklike arms held him in a strong grip. He turned a body aside with his clenched hand and, choked by the reek of sweat and dust, struggled free from his first captor. A riflebutt sent a stab of pain through his back, though he evaded the full blow by an accidental swerve. He struck out wildly, aided by a sudden flashback of animal strength that, used thus towards positive ends, cancelled out those opposite gulfs of panic to which such thoughtless action was not too distantly allied.

There was no option of surrender: they were swamped in a planned rush by the soldiers whose main intent was to kill for sport and loot at leisure. Evart went down, pulled by the legs, feeling the earth's blackness close over him. He struggled blindly to stay conscious, while at the same time hoping to hear the crack of rifleshots as an indication that the massacre had begun and the misery ended.

Machine gun fire was followed by a voice shouting orders. It melted the hard grip of plunderers' hands, caused them to break off in the middle of unconscious actions, to

31

disentangle themselves from the orchestra and, though against the grain of their unseeing passionless eyes, to form rough lines some distance off. Two men with blood-smeared faces crept away from Armgardson; there was the sound of a man trying to stop himself sobbing – which sounded worse than any sobbing – and then there was silence. Evart stood up slowly and wiped blood from a graze on his hand. No one seemed badly hurt: they gathered by the heap of boxes, some of whose lids had been smashed by riflebutts or prized by the more cunning with bayonets.

The officer who fired the shots pushed a gangway through the soldiers and, rough tactician that he was, placed himself between them and the orchestra. His highly polished boots and neat uniform were a pleasing and promising contrast to the rabble-like appearance of the soldiers, who looked bitterly at the lost prize of the orchestra, and were unable to understand now why they had not attacked sooner. Several moved forward, pressing on the safety-catch of their arms, and the officer shouted in a strong clear voice, obviously threatening them if they came closer. Evart and the others stood still, watching his brilliant confidence before what seemed great danger, feeling perfectly safe under his charge, even though no one understood what he was saying. He looked at his watch, then at the soldiers, and bellowed another sentence at them. They were calmer, though still unable to give up the thought of how easily they had lost such a magnificent prize. He loosened his revolver when a sudden movement broke out in the ranks. Some of the soldiers unslung their rifles.

He called out once more, yet at the same time, despite the angry tone of his voice, he smiled at them, and his smile was based on the same set of facial muscles as when he shouted his menacing orders. He was a huge man, like a handsome and tremendous schoolboy blessed with a

32

command of mature petulance, and his illogical and unpre-dictable actions obviously came from a mind that was unconscious of this humorous and impetuous trait. He pulled the revolver from his belt and cocked it, laughing as if at the novelty of having to use it.

They started to come forward, their ranks bending in the centre, unwilling on either flank. With a roar of baffled rage the centre broke, and several soldiers stood in the open, their bony elongated faces rigid, their grey-blue eyes fixed on the members and luggage-piles of the orchestra. The officer drew back, snatched the machine gun from his orderly and play-acted with it, pushing one foot forward and pressing the gun into his side, then pulling back and going forward again, miming the actions of spraying mutineers with bullets. This lasted barely a minute. Whether from fatigue or impatience, or ill-judgement (for it seemed that his actions hypnotized them or at least made them reflect) he stepped back to await developments. He was smiling widely as if he had enjoyed the performance which, it now turned out, had succeeded neither in hypnotic effect nor as a warning, for one of the soldiers came too close. The steel butt of the gun smashed against his head, and only at the impact was the smile seen to leave the officer's face.

Without trying any more tricks, he opened fire. The rapid crack-crack-crack turned them into frenzied dancers, then acrobats as they twisted grotesquely and fell, wounded and dying on the stones. The only detail that emerged later from the general feeling of horror was the fact that during the actual firing, when bullets were entering living flesh, no cries were uttered from the soldiers. The stick-magazine was emptied and fell also, and the officer stamped on it with his boot, as if to crush it for becoming so quickly useless. There was a lull in the heavy guns from the hills, and sounds of peace came to life again, even to the forlorn singing of a few birds.

No one in the orchestra spoke or moved. Evart was numbed at having witnessed a primeval monster amputating with its own teeth a limb that would not properly function. The Gorshek officer set pickets around the orchestra and dismissed the rest of the company to a clump of trees nearby. He motioned Evart to sit down, explaining to Starnberg in German that lorries would come soon to take them to the headquarters' village. Soldiers, as emissaries, approached the officer, who agreed that they could take away their wounded, on condition that they buried the dead. They stood out of sight, below the level of a bank, and gunfire drowned the groans of the wounded and the sound of mattocks attacking the stony soil.

Hope had completely gone from the orchestra. (To be saved in such a way from death seemed to Evart merely a marked postponement of their own. The world was given over to such men as this officer who, without philosophy for his actions, was applying his hands to philosophical murder: an old-fashioned Hegelian superman killing Peter so as to be able to kill Paul later.) They sat or lay like men more than lost: men who did not speak or hope or think back to when hope had been possible, or think forward to when it might be possible once more. Since they were here already, hope had never been possible, and since the officer had so thoughtlessly killed his own soldiers it seemed that hope would never be felt by them again.

They sat smoking, some talking, most looking at the officer who stood with legs astride before them – as if he were a god in whom they had lost faith. A few did nothing, curiously listened to the rising and dying of the bombardment: on one crescendo the volume of sound rose higher and higher, like an increasing tremor that threatened to split the earth, and when it apparently reached the height of its power there was a quick second of silence, a splinter of visionary time stolen from the kingdom of noise.

Then the guns came again all at once and went full-powered for one desperate half minute like the last terrible sound of a dying monster. Then they stopped, suddenly and, it seemed, for no reason.

Starnberg was talking to the officer, using a broken childhood grammar of German. A cigarette was declined, and he considered this an unpropitious beginning. 'I don't smoke either,' he explained, 'but I carry this packet for friends. It helps conversation.'

'Do your friends smoke, then?' he was asked.

'Can't you see them?'

The officer looked around. 'Is it because they're nervous?'

'I think so.' Starnberg had difficulty in looking into his face, and when he did so he saw that it was not a cruel face; but then he thought of how he had shot down his own soldiers.

'Why are they nervous?' the officer wanted to know.

It seemed to Starnberg that he only spoke from an empty and indolent curiosity, and perhaps a simple desire to show off his knowledge of another language. 'The war makes them nervous. And the fact that they're prisoners.'

The officer could not understand. 'But why does that make them nervous?'

'They think they'll be killed.' He watched closely for the response to this.

The officer's eyes twinkled, and he smiled. 'It isn't necessary that they be afraid.'

Starnberg did not want to ask anything else, having discovered what he had been probing to find out, but he extended his arm to the sound of the firing: 'Why is there still so much noise?'

'Your guns are trying to stop our soldiers,' the officer said with a smile, tapping the revolver in his belt.

'Will they succeed?'

'Yes. You have too much artillery. But after the winter we will break through. Our General is too clever for you.'

'Perhaps you will,' Starnberg said wearily. A column of heavy, troop-carrying lorries came along the road, and soldiers by the trees began walking to where they would stop. 'These are for you,' the officer said, adding that the orchestra was to climb inside and be taken to the village.

The arrival of the lorries was a relief, a reason for moving out of the dust and smoke and paralysing uncertainty of what was going to happen. Queues of even length formed quickly at the back of each one, an armed soldier behind every line like the poisonous sting in the tail of a scorpion, ready to go into action should anything move out of place. Instruments and luggage were lifted carefully up behind them and the wooden lorry-backs fastened securely with steel pins. Engines roared, the officer swung himself on to the last truck, and the convoy moved off under the hot sun of midday, leaving no trace of their capture on the pebbled expanse of earth except an uneven mound of half buried soldiers – above which black birds with enormous wingspan and sickle beaks floated gracefully.

Evart, smoking a cigarette, still lived in the careless non-chalance of a dream. Though sometimes jolted out of it at the sharp angle of a crossroads, it always returned when steady vibrations took the lorry again along the flat. The thin thread which so many men thought divided them from cowardice was often far wider and stronger than they imagined. It was only by this aphorism that he could explain his feeling of indifference to all that had happened in the last few hours. Yet fear was somewhere in him, he realized, a blacker and deadlier fear perhaps than the others might feel; but it was more a hidden panic, of which he was only aware by a slight physical nervousness, and a momentary sensation of complete mind-emptiness. If the emptiness was ever filled, it could only be filled by fear. To himself, he divided fear into two classes: fear of death, which included fear of physical pain; and a universal fear for the death of something 'other than himself. But Starnberg, who sat beside him on the planked seating like a ubiquitous shadow, intervened with a question:

'What do you think our chances are?'

Evart looked at him: 'Of what exactly?'

'Living.'

'Reasonable.'

Other men listened, their hearts ready to leap on to any favourable oracle. 'Why should we be in danger?' he went on. 'We aren't soldiers. The officers in the village may be more civilized than the rabble we've just seen.' My tolerance speaking, tolerance towards people who are afraid. Why do I lie? Because I can't trust them? Or because I can't trust myself? He shrugged his shoulders, clutched the support-bars of the lorry as it jumped over a rut. If I were afraid like the others I might be able to help them. The sky gap at the end of the covered lorry was a hot, empty blue, like anywhere in the world: timeless and spaceless, the universal eye that would look upon them to the end of their journey. At the back of each lorry was a Gorshek guard, a rifle and fixed bayonet outlined as a marker to their destination. The life and death of my orchestra. Bayonet and violin, woodwinds and rifles, bombshells and screaming brass. In the past, he said to himself, whole civilizations have gone under water, taking language, music, literature, everything with it. It's the same with us. The music that we ensure is remembered can be gradually sucked out of the air and destroyed. Is this important? Music will become known again after several centuries. Different music though. But what does this matter? Would the prospect of it going for ever bother me? The agony was not caused by the fact that music, like writing, could suddenly vanish from the earth, but because he could not decide whether such a thing would matter to him. He found himself staring out of the lorry, at the brown dry soil of the lane unfolding below.

He looked up at the faces opposite, wanting to know what each would say when it opened its mouth. The even vibration of the lorry gave their eyes a look of dull weariness, as if they had been several days without sleep, and too long with neither hope nor life. The lorry engine was so loud that they could not make the necessary effort to talk above it. The same expressionless weariness marked Starnberg's face, eyes turned inwards to their own fatigue, and Evart wondered if he himself looked similarly dazed to the others. They were passing groups of huddled, wooden houses on the outskirts of a large village.

He was suddenly pulled and tugged by the empty air, and laid a hand on Starnberg's shoulder to stop himself falling. The lorries parked before a large house, and their backs were unlatched so that they could climb down. Evart stretched his arms and yawned. Starnberg seemed afraid to jump, and those behind grumbled at him to make haste, so Evart took his arm and steadied him as he let go of the bar.

'Here at last,' Evart said. 'I wonder where we'll live?' Starnberg looked around. Work parties were clearing rubble from a demolished house across the road and had taken most of their clothes off in the sun's heat. Much of the village was in ruins, and the wide road leading to the centre was bordered by undulating lines of collapsed telegraph poles. The noise of a motor cycle at full throttle ripped through the dusty air. Staff cars were arriving and departing from the space before the house every few seconds, throwing up clouds of stifling grey powder that seemed to be emitted from secret reservoirs in each wheel. A group of officers stood talking by the porch, were mournfully observed by a skeleton-like dog from the steps.

The Gorshek officer ordered the lorries away, and approached Evart. 'While you're here,' he said, pointing, 'your party are to stay in that barn. My soldiers will help you in with your luggage, and food will be brought in half an hour. Later you'll be taken to see the General.'

He turned to give orders to the soldiers who had stood silent and vacant-eyed, and they began lifting instrument and luggage boxes, carrying them into the barn across the road. They opened the tall ramshackle doors, and Evart led the orchestra inside.

3

After swallowing two bicarbonate pills while still at the dining-room table the General waited patiently for the relief of eructation. What objects remained on the table – wine bottles, dessert cutlery, glasses, cigar case – became as clear as if illuminated in a saint's vision, and what began as a burn in the stomach suddenly leapt into his throat.

'Better,' he said with more normal consciousness, 'better.' Another belch came and, with a smile, he poured an extra allowance of brandy. Feeling a movement at his elbow he leaned to one side so that his servant could take away the coffee cup – the captured house had been rich with the civilized provender in which the enemy excelled – and he stretched out his short gaitered legs until his feet rested on the wooden centre-bar beneath the table. While the General smoked, phrases came into his mind on which he would build the day's communiqué for High Command:

'A lightning advance during the morning of thirty-five miles, bringing our forces in consolidated strength to the foothills of the enemy's main defensive range. The enemy bridgehead on our side of the mountains, which he thought to hold for the winter and break out from in the spring, was contained, smashed and thrown back by our troops so successfully that the overall tactical position on this front has been considerably altered in our favour.'

The music of sporadic shellfire played him into complete serenity. Feeling a tightness at his tunic belt he unhooked three eyeholes and sighed at the relieving slackness.

'Twenty-three villages captured along a front of fifty miles. Numberless casualties inflicted. Hundreds of tanks

40

and motor vehicles destroyed and captured. Full accounts in next few hours. Own casualties medium to heavy. New headquarters established in agreed position.'

The high spirits of his soldiers outside the house blended pleasantly with the richness of his well-being. He moved a hand slowly down to the ashtray and tapped his cigar on its rim, so that a barrel of ash fell away intact and rested on its polished base. He stared at it for some seconds, then let his thumb slide and crush it to powder.

'The object of this limited offensive was to open a clear road for the final attack in the spring. While not too exposed by enemy harassing in their winter positions, our troops will (1) draw enemy counter-attacks upon them and so bleed their reinforcement battlegroups, and (2) maintain the strength of their forward positions for the spring offensive, the object of which will be the old capital. This will entail a drive of a thousand miles across the main range, the southern rivers, and the plains . . .'

He expanded on the intricacies of a sound strategic plan. Perhaps he would write an essay, deliver it as a lecture to the staff officers during the slack months of winter. Yes, a good idea. He would have maps drawn to illustrate the main direction of attack, and obtain graphs from the logistics department to show the rate of build-up necessary before it could take place.

'The surprise element of the offensive was due to the failure of the enemy's intelligence system, and also to a newly worked-out method of advancing troops in mass under camouflage to points fifty miles behind the lines and then into forest ten miles behind the lines, and finally transporting them to the forward trenches in tunnels excavated several months ago by labour battalions beneath the fields. Huge underground assembly points were built so that tanks and men could gather in mass for a sudden breakout straight into the enemy lines. Thus by arduous preparation a tactical victory was won, a victory that will lead to a strategic breakout and advance in the coming spring.'

His lecture would be followed by the actual offensive, and the details appeared simple and deadly as soon as they had occurred to him, a triumph of the persistent, intelligent conduct of war: 'Four diversionary attacks will be made. (1) 25 miles north of the actual place to be broken through. This the enemy will easily recognize as a feint. (2) In the actual place to be broken through, which will also seem a feint. (3) Into the main road–railway pass through the mountains, which will take the enemy by surprise and cause him to think it another of my novel and daring moves, and therefore the real one. (4) The breakthrough as stated in 2. This sector will have become quiet, and the attack will be launched while number 3 feint is still in progress. Timing and logistics must be accurately worked out for these moves.'

Later he would write a more intellectual essay theorizing on the powers of artistic imagination employed in the pursuit of war. It might even form the theme of a short book, an emblematic crown to his previous journals, a volume that would doubtlessly be incorporated into the staff-officers' syllabus, printed and reprinted by the state. He could think of no greater reward for his selfless dedication to the art of war.

'The triple-pronged drive followed unique directional lines, and was completely successful.' His mind elaborated on labyrinthine tactical exercises until the sun crept across his brandy glass and he began to doze. He saw the glory of his career standing before him on a shining cliff, on whose sheer surface arrows coiled and darted over maps where the attainment of some objective was marked at the end of each decisive line.

Suddenly he woke up. Ash fell from his cigar and broke into powder on the knee of his grey uniform. Brushing it away he looked at the chronograph on his wrist. Fifteen thirty. He had not slept for three days. The luxurious after-dinner tiredness turned into fatigue so he pushed his chair away, yawned, and stretched himself, feeling some clarity come back into his eyes, and rheumatic aches beginning to leave his shoulders. Pulling the rumpled cloth of his tunic straight he walked in short steps towards the door that led to his office, which he entered with strides of dignity.

The walls were covered with maps. Huge patches of green forest edged the feet of purple layer-tinted mountains; inked-in cities of industrial areas were webbed and fastened together by roads and railways; while vast plains in the south stood empty, but for scattered nomad villages and silk-blue skeins of dying lakeland, that were bordered and ignored by the cotton-thin windings of erratic rivers. Between the window-inset and the wall-corner hung a long sheet of explanatory data, like columns of coloured symbols on a temple prayer sheet, with elaborate scales and marginal instructions for magnetic variation. On the door hung a chart of divisional strengths under his command, neatly subdivided into numbered regiments and battalions. Three field telephones had been installed on a plain wooden desk, and the papers were laid out in labelled stacks. A single picture hung by the door: that of a Gorshek hero long since dead, placed in every army headquarters by order of High Command.

He closed the door, and the presence of surrounding maps filled him with a sense of poetic veneration. Walking from one wall to another he was shrewdly entranced by the beauty of their design, calculatingly fascinated by the black curving railways and the differing geometrical shapes of stretches of plain and forest land. Nothing could mar the beauty of topographical maps, he said to himself; they were faultless representations of the earth's surface, with all the numerous marks of man's and nature's accomplishments set plainly upon them.

He sat in the armchair behind his desk, still tired, yet

43

eased by the sense of achievement that his latest clever and overwhelming offensive had given him. He was perusing the first lists of casualty returns when a knock sounded at the door.

'Come in,' he shouted.

The door opened and closed, and he heard between his swift calculations strides across the tiled floor, then a rush of air and the brush of a hand on uniform cloth as it came down from a salute. Having assessed the total of one division's casualties, he demanded, without looking up:

'Well?'

'Captain Kondal, your excellency.'

He moved the papers to one side. The appearance of the officer pleased him, his height, his shaven face that was as content as it could be without actually smiling, his clean well-pressed uniform, and the complete aura emanating from him, saying that even he had his little accomplishments to feel pleased about. He pointed to a chair. 'What is it? Sit down then, Kondal.'

He obeyed, saying: 'Your excellency, this morning, on my way back from the advanced position, I took some prisoners.'

The General drew in his feet so that they rested beneath the chair, drum-tapped on his desk with a pencil, and tried to focus his mind on this novelty thrown up at the tail end of his campaign. 'Prisoners?' he said with a puzzled, annoyed frown.

The officer sensed his irritation. 'Yes, your excellency, they were . . .'

'How many?' the General broke in.

'Ninety-three, your excellency.'

His pencil fell, rolled on to the floor. 'Leave it be,' he said sharply, looking across at him. 'You know that no prisoners are ever taken. Taking prisoners causes unnecessary complications. If we took prisoners we'd need half our army to guard them, and prisoners never work, so they are

44

no use at all. Taking prisoners is an old-fashioned way of making war.' Which is another subject I may mention in my book.

'I thought these prisoners would be useful for interrogation, your excellency.'

'You shouldn't think beyond the rules laid down for you,' he cried. 'In any case, I have my own methods of gathering intelligence. And besides, soldiers never have the knowledge to give useful information, and those who have never put themselves in a position to be captured.'

Still blindly convinced he had acted rightly, the officer told him: 'These prisoners are different, your excellency.'

The General laughed ironically. 'All prisoners have to be fed, housed and guarded. Only if your prisoners are so special as not to need these things can they be different.'

Sitting with his hands pressed on to his knees, the officer waited for him to say something else.

'Well, what sort of prisoners are they?'

'They're some orchestra whose train came through our attack,' he said, speaking quickly. 'The tanks had just gone by, and I saw their train when the smoke cleared. I suppose they were going to play to their soldiers. Our men wanted to kill them when they got out of the train, but I didn't think they should be killed.' His explanation limped and stumbled, became incoherent, and he stopped speaking as if he suddenly did not know why he hadn't killed the prisoners.

The General's equanimity was touched by a tremor-like disturbance. 'How do you know they were members of an orchestra?'

'They had musical instruments, your excellency.'

He picked up another pencil and rolled it in the palm of his hand. 'Where are they now?'

'Locked in the barn.'

The General's breath hissed out like steam: a symphony orchestra taken prisoner. What Kondal told him made a

45

fold on the reflected glory of his smooth attack, unsteadied his fluidity of purpose. The wildest imaginative conceptions of war did not embrace the capture of a symphony orchestra. High Command were right: the easiest way out of any problem was to kill; yet an intellectual curiosity made him ponder: perhaps he should interrogate the man in charge and see what he could discover, militarily or otherwise, instead of following High Command's orders that had been laid down since the war's beginning and having them shot at once. Under pretext of interrogation he could keep them alive for a few hours. The officer stood, hoping to be dismissed. 'The barn in the field, across the road?' he was asked.

'Yes, your excellency.'

'How many were killed by the train?'

'None, your excellency. They were lucky. The soldiers were about to kill them when I arrived.'

Echoes of his previous mood returned, and the maps on the wall held the triumphant and comforting spirit of the morning's battle around him like a silk-lined airtight cocoon. 'Good,' he said complacently. 'I'm glad they weren't.' He saw the pleasure in his subordinate's face. 'And Captain Kondal,' he went on, 'I'll want to see the conductor of the orchestra in ten minutes.' Kondal saluted, turned precisely about, and strode towards the door with relief. The General had a further thought: 'Captain?'

He turned and saluted, but without coming forward. 'Yes, your excellency?'

'See that the barn is well guarded. No one must escape.'

'Yes, your excellency.' He went out, closing the door quietly.

The General was alone once more with his maps, casualty lists, divisional organization charts, and the portrait of the Gorshek hero hanging to the left of the door. Pictures of the dead should be discarded, he thought, looking at it; they should not expect people to be stared at by the faces

46

of those who had died. If anything could be said to disturb the perfect contentment of his mind at this moment it was the bland half smiling half young face of this tall upright man on which the régime had prospered, the sort of person who would one day be in control, and who would eventually come to lack the imagination even to keep a war going. The General was somewhat surpised that he should have these thoughts. Were they a condition of success? he asked himself with a smile. Yet they seemed unimportant compared to the balance of power held by his maps on the wall's coverage.

He opened a drawer by his knee and took out a box of cigarettes, considered lighting one, but laid the box down and began writing on a signal pad:

'The last phases of the advance are complete. Our forces are established in strength before the hills of the enemy's winter lines in anticipation for a quick breakthrough in the spring. Enemy casualties conservatively estimated at thirty thousand men killed. Five hundred tanks destroyed. One hundred and thirty destroyed after capture. Two thousand motor vehicles destroyed. Three hundred destroyed after capture. Four hundred guns destroyed. Fifty destroyed after capture. Other figures awaited.'

He looked at the impressive list and, reaching for a pencil, inserted between the last two sentences: 'Passenger train captured, with locomotive. Destroyed.' The message was signed with a quick flourish, and when he rang the bell on his desk an orderly entered and took the signal out for transmission. The General lit a cigarette and, with his arms before him on the desk, sat in a position of habitual alertness which nevertheless allowed for some meditation. The seeming fantasy of the orchestra's capture brought his imagination into contact with his commonsense, mechanical mind, and he became somewhat curious, though not stirred beyond this, so that he was left still with only a military problem. He did not ask what was to be done with the ninety-three men, assuming quite safely that such a question would be answered when he had seen the conductor of the orchestra, knowing that in war there were no extra-military experiences, that even the beggars that made themselves a nuisance in every newly occupied town presented a problem that could immediately be dealt with by the art of war. The capture of a symphony orchestra, a great intellectual instrument of entertainment, prophesied little more than a minor action by his military machine.

4

There was a strong smell of recent animal habitation. Bales of hay were stacked around wooden walls and a ladder in a corner led to a loft above. A row of storm lamps, shaped like booths at a fair, stood on a shelf, and rusting horse-harness hung on a far wall to the left of a barred window. Behind a stack of hay was a broken plough, and by the door a pyramid of newly seasoned woodplanks. 'At least we'll be comfortable,' Evart remarked, as the doors were fastened and locked behind them. 'Quite a pleasant prison.'

'Until the winter sets in,' Bender said, who overheard, 'then we'll freeze to death.'

'I don't think we'll be here by then,' Viccadi put in ambiguously. They sat on bales of hay, talking in sharply defined groups, according to the different instrument sections of the orchestra to which they belonged. Evart, who had been standing by himself, walked to the group occupying the hay by the closed door. He spoke to the men standing up: Armgardson who played the piccolo and bass flute, a tall man dressed in navy-blue. Everyone in the orchestra called him 'Two-metres', which pleased him because he was proud of his height. He had steel blue eyes and sleek blond hair, and was already inclined to obesity, of which he was not proud.

'How are you feeling?' Evart asked.

No one knew how they were feeling. Only Armgardson was decisive. 'I hope we'll be leaving this place soon,' he said in a deep voice. 'I don't think the idea of staying here appeals to me.'

This too obvious complaint brought laughter from the

others. 'We got into it suddenly enough,' Evart replied, 'so perhaps we shall get out of it with the same speed.'

'I feel that the quicker you get into a situation the harder it is to escape from it,' a trombone player contended, languidly sprawled over a heap of softened hay.

'If nothing happens soon,' Armgardson said, 'I'll make my own way back. I'll get out of this, I tell you.'

Starnberg fastened the buttons of his coat. One was missing from the fight by the train, so he loosened it and sat down, sighing a sigh that might equally have been for the loss of the button as for his loss of freedom.

'The others don't seem too disturbed,' Evart said.

'Give them time,' Starnberg answered resentfully, as if his own sensibility were in question. 'They haven't thought about it yet. The shock's still with them. They're quiet now, aren't they? But the shock's going, so you'll see their reactions soon, when they remember the torture stories from newspapers and magazines, all the bloody gory stuff we've been shown for years and years. Their sensations are dull and void at the moment, but watch them when they wake up later, which they're bound to do. If they get the chance.'

Evart broke in to stop him. 'They'll have the chance,' he snapped. 'I don't think anything like that'll happen. The big danger was at the train, and we're out of it now.'

'I heard they never took prisoners,' Starnberg said thoughtfully.

Evart reassured him. 'If they're not soldiers they do.'

Starnberg needed more convincing. 'You can depend on nothing,' he said.

'You have to think you can, or go mad.'

'So unless that happens we'll be prisoners for good?'

Evart was ironic. 'Until we're liberated.'

Starnberg raised his voice. '*If* we're liberated.' Then he asked: 'Do you really think we'll get out of this soon?'

'When we've won the war.'

Such quiet cynicism made him happy. 'Do you think we'll win the war?' he asked with a broad smile.

'Why not? We've been told for the last four years that we'll win it. Why disbelieve them?' Unable to find his matches he put away the cigarette he had thought to light.

Starnberg did not smile. 'And the Gorsheks have been told for the last four years that they'll win.'

'Aren't you a gambler? Don't you ever spin coins up to see whether there's a God or not? Don't you make bets with yourself as to whether or not you'll be alive next week? You should. It makes living so much more interesting.'

'Be serious,' Starnberg said. 'There's too much to lose to turn gambler. Unfortunately we're unable to gamble about anything. All the gambling's been done.'

'Even so,' Evart smiled. 'There's not much to lose. Life has become cheap again: they've been pushing that fact on to us for years, while the truth is that life's always been cheap. Except where an orchestra is concerned. That's a different thing. The theory of it being killed has always appalled me, and now we're staring the possibility of it in the face.'

Starnberg answered, raising his voice: 'I know what you mean. But I can't think about that yet, because my personal fear gets in the way. Theories don't get much of a chance to come out of me at a time like this. I can't face physical violence. I'm frightened. At the train I couldn't fight back. I became passive and waited for them to kill me. It's a trick of one's ancestry, a trick that lies low and waits for a time like this: then lets you down.' He looked up, half expecting to find contempt on Evart's face. But he saw indifference. 'I'd rather be a coward, than not feel anything,' he cried out. 'I want the lid off my feelings so that I know what makes me work, so that I can feel some life in me.' Talking gave him comfort, and he turned against Evart to continue it: 'Bravery is a state of mind, that's all. And bravery's stupidity if it costs you your life,

51

or your ability to feel.' His grey eyes suddenly sharpened: 'It's only your state of mind that makes you stay so calm,' he said, and walked back to the others.

Evart stood alone, with nothing to do or say or to prophesy. He leaned against a bale of hay, his fingers clutching his face, refusing the physical sedative of a cigarette. Thoughts crashed the outer rim of his mind: the fact that nothing could save the orchestra cut a deep groove in him. There was no way of saving them: he could give nothing in exchange for their lives – poverty being most painful when your life was worthless – and there was not even some Being worse than the Devil to whom he could sell his soul in exchange for their lives. The Devil had already filled himself by purchasing the souls of the Gorsheks who had captured them (so the propagandists stated), and had become replete on those who had sent them. Every value was inflated until none existed. They were gripped by the same blind force of evil and power that had always haunted so many of his dreams. In his mind he heard the black procession of their prophesied deaths, the futile fact of their disappearance, a coronach sinking into a rimless lake whose words would tell an uncomprehending world that they had once lived. No one would know, and it would make little difference if they did.

Sounds of motor-traffic, and men shouting orders and rabble exulting in the afternoon sun reached him from the road. He heard the bark of a dog and a dull crash in the distance of an unsafe building, and from farther away came the softened intonation of gunfire. The members of the orchestra, still in their sharply divided groups, did not seem particularly disturbed, but talked amiably among themselves. Fear and anxiety cannot last for ever, he thought. We are not given that much dignity. It degenerates either to indifference or a false contentment. Two trumpet players who had produced a pack of cards were

52

making a rough planked table from the wood in the corner. Others were reading; some were gathering hay for a bed.

There was nothing to do and nothing to say. The word 'hope' came like a silver arrow into his thoughts, but went away on the wings of its own ineptitude, leaving no trace because of an unimpeded flight. They had been prisoners for a few hours, yet it seemed as if they had never been anything else but prisoners. If you die as a prisoner you have always been a prisoner, imprisoned in a corridor leading you to that fate, and time is a line on which you travel to reach it. If only I could do something. The words were necessary, but useless, like numbered dice against a closed box. So what was the point in shaking them around?

The doors opened. Sunlight and noise came in, followed by two guards with food. He watched some of the others go towards them, excited at the prospect of eating. They shared the food, ladling stew into deep tin plates, and when the bucket was empty, the guards went out for more.

Leaning against a bale of hay he lit a cigarette. At four o'clock two armed guards and the officer who had saved them by the train came to take him to the General's office for interrogation.

5

A field telephone vibrated loudly and startled him from his thoughts. Leaning forward he lifted its receiver: 'The signal has been transmitted, your excellency,' he heard. Ah! the wireless section. 'Thank you,' he said, and put the receiver down. The slow step of tired soldiers sounded out of the window behind him, and a sudden crescendo of motor-traffic swamped the murmur of the afternoon bombardment. As he listened for other sounds, a knock came at the door.

'The prisoner is here, your excellency,' Kondal said.

'Bring him in. The guards can stay outside.'

Kondal retired. There was a ringing sound as the guards brought their rifles to rest on the stone floor of the hall, and when the door opened again the General saw the conductor of the orchestra standing in the room, with Kondal tapping him on the back as a sign that he should go forward.

The General stood up.

Evart walked slowly across the space between the door and the desk. He was asked to sit down. He looked at the General calmly, seeing a short bald man standing behind a desk, surrounded by a natural complement of walled maps, a uniformed figure vanguarded by a trio of ebony telephones. His truculent blue eyes looked straight at Evart. There was a smile on his lips, and his firm chin lifted as he ordered Kondal to remain by the door. Smiles creased the skin at the corners of his eyes. 'I hear you were going to play before your soldiers at the front?'

'We were,' Evart replied.

The General smiled. 'And now you find that there is no front?'

'Not exactly. It only seems to have moved a few miles,' came the sharp retort.

The General's eyes twinkled. 'Quite right. But perhaps you can tell me where it's moved to?'

Evart turned to walk out of the room, but saw Kondal standing at the door, an imperturbable statue against which he stood no chance. He swung around to face the General: 'You're a soldier. You have maps. You should know,' he snapped.

'The hills to the east?' the General questioned.

Evart's lips grew tight in an expression of disgust. 'One thing I lack is an accurate sense of topography.'

The General wrote something on a sheet of paper. 'A pity,' he said. 'But why don't you sit down?' he added solicitously. 'It makes talking much easier.'

'When there's something to talk about, I agree.' He waved his arm towards the maps. 'I know nothing about all this.'

'Then you should find it so much more interesting,' the General suggested. 'Maps are the anatomical charts of war.'

Evart could not resist an answer. 'Only of war? Your definition is wrong: anatomical charts are used for healing; they help a surgeon to cure wounds of the body, whereas your maps help to make those wounds. There's nothing interesting in war.'

The General opened a box of cigarettes and passed it to him. 'On the contrary,' he denied. 'Allow me to tell you that I've spent many years deciding what war is. It's the art of decimation. It is also nature's way of filling the empty sack-bag of men's ideals; it puts a machine gun into their hands when a theory has been pushed to the limits of their intelligence.'

Evart looked up sharply. Despite the General's cynicism

55

he was aware for the first time since his capture of talking to a human being of the 'other side'. It was momentarily felt by both as if they had known each other before, or recognized behind each face certain character traits that each knew in some vague way he possessed himself. It could not be acknowledged to each other, and in any case would have done no good, for it may well have been as much a basis for enmity as friendship. But Evart was disturbed by this almost subconscious affinity he felt to the General; while the General accepted it as a kind of sympathy for each other, an added piquancy that could in no way deflect him from his intention of killing the prisoner and his orchestra.

'You seem surprised that there's so much to it!' the General said affably. 'Well, there's plenty more. War gives men an excuse for leaving an intolerable situation without hurting their pride: it's a cover for cowardice. Don't you agree?'

Evart did agree.

'That's one way of looking at it, at any rate,' the General went on. 'Yet it's even more than that. To me it's an artistic way of making sure that my nation survives.'

'Survives what?' Evart could not resist asking.

'Your nation,' he said with simple conviction. 'You can put all the theories of the world into the earth and blow them up with dynamite, but one thing will still be there: power, the power of one nation over another, the simple dog-eat-dog of nation against nation each fighting for what they call freedom. My country's fighting like mad to break and conquer your country; and your country is bleeding itself to death trying to ruin mine. You call it freedom. We call it survival. As a soldier I'm not so interested in the difference between these two reasons, false or true as they might be. I merely call war an art, an interesting thing.' He was surprised at his own animation. What a fool I am, he said to himself. Why do I try to justify myself before this stranger?

Evart suspected a trick. Their methods of investigation, he had read, often began by something that resembled a confession from your interrogator so that you would stumble out more easily with your own. 'Well, I can't tell you anything about it,' he said, but accepted a cigarette as he sat down.

The General smiled. 'You've told me a lot already.'

'Nothing you didn't previously know.'

He blew a shaft of blue smoke across the casualty reports, stood up and walked to a map. 'You've told me,' he said, tracing a line along purple contours with his finger, 'that your army still has its main defences on the range of hills you came through this morning, instead of behind the river twenty miles eastward.'

Evart looked down at the smoke winding from the end of his cigarette. 'I've told you nothing, and you know it.'

'I'm afraid you have. Why did you allow me to extract the information so easily? We usually have much more trouble.' The centre telephone rang. He said into the mouthpiece: 'I'll be free at six o'clock' – and put it down.

'Because I have no interest in war,' Evart replied. 'My instincts are more peaceful, and therefore civilized.'

'But don't you believe that your army is fighting for your civilization?' the General asked suavely, stubbing out his cigarette before sitting down to face him again.

Evart stared at him in anger. 'I've told you,' he reiterated, 'I don't believe in war, no matter what problems have to be solved. Problems that have to be solved by war aren't legitimate problems at all.'

'You have very definite opinions,' the General said sympathetically. 'But look at it from our point of view. Hasn't it ever occurred to you that we aren't trying to settle any problems by this war? War isn't the place for problems. And neither is war a social necessity with us, as it seemed to be with you – I beg your pardon, with the side you happen, against your will of course, to be on. War is and always has been mainly an expression of timeless atavism' – he lost patience here and came out with a more colourful and expedite image: 'the boils in man's nature feeling the occasional necessity of suppuration.'

Evart noted the slight shifting of the General's statements. It may be a trick, he thought, though a useless one because I've nothing to hide. 'You've given much thought to the subject of war,' he said with some sarcasm.

'It requires much thought. War deserves a complete philosophy.'

'Philosophy is the pursuit of wisdom,' he retorted.

'Philosophy is the pursuit of knowledge,' the General told him.

The two statements sounded, and were, implacable. The silence they commanded was broken by Evart. 'If it's the knowledge you've just acquired from me, then I've suffered no loss.' He leaned forward in the chair and brushed back his greying hair. Seeing the General smile he said with open irony: 'Your philosophy at any rate seems to be an amusing subject. I don't find war amusing.'

'A layman's remarks are, though,' the General quietly scoffed. Evart did not reply, but took another cigarette and lit it. The General, who found the conversation stimulating, leaned forward to the desk and rested his arms along its edge: 'Don't you believe that your army is fighting for your freedom?'

The reply was emphatic. 'No army ever fought for anybody's freedom.'

'But you love freedom, don't you?' the General went on, brushing a fly from his forehead.

'I love the idea of it.'

'Don't you believe it exists?'

Evart rested back in his chair, relinquishing his unnecessary position of alertness. 'Not during a war, certainly.'

'But what about before? Didn't you have freedom then?'

'It took them fifteen years to prepare us for the war, which was plenty of time for it to have gone out of fashion,' he contested wearily.

'And after the war?'

'They will have forgotten the feeling of it.'

'Then you think the war is going to end?'

'It must, if only to rest a while and prepare for the next one.'

The General was enjoying the conversation, which was bound by no rigid political rules and was not hurried to its finish by a timid opponent. 'But don't you believe there'll be any freedom left in the world?' he asked.

Evart leaped up, crying out: 'What do you mean? Freedom! Why do you keep on using such a false and stupid word? Freedom, freedom, freedom! Listen to it. Doesn't it have a meaningless sound? It's been twisted, hammered, burned and dragged inside-out. It's caused so much suffering in the world in these many disguises for tyranny that the sooner people forget that it ever existed the better.'

The General remained calm, determined to carry on the argument in a pleasant manner. 'I don't agree. If the word has no meaning for you, then you've only yourself to blame, and I'm sorry for you. It has a most definite meaning for me.'

'Of course, if there's still such a thing as freedom it's only possessed by dictators and people like you,' Evart said angrily.

The General felt suddenly annoyed. 'Every man's answerable to someone, and so am I, believe it or not. Dictators are by no means free. You're wrong there. Only the workers have freedom these days, and that's very limited, for their own benefit. It's a compromise that keeps those in power who want to stay in power.' He saw Evart not listening, looking down at a vacant spot on the floor, his forehead furrowed with deep creases. There was a length of ash on his cigarette so that the heat was almost touching his fingers. He suddenly looked up, and the ash fell on to the floor. The General did not feel any more annoyance. 'Tell me,' he said, 'when did your orchestra last perform?'

Evart leaned forward, placed his cigarette in the ashtray. 'Two thousand years ago,' he replied.

The General laughed. 'Where? In Pompeii?'

'No, in Madrid. And by time it was only ten weeks ago. If you want to know the only time when people possess complete freedom, it's during the few hours they listen to music.'

'Possibly. But what sort of people are they? They're mice, I tell you. They aren't you and they aren't me. I play as well, and people listen. My music may be a different kind, but it's listened to just the same. Whose side are you on now?'

Evart felt utter disgust at this cheap attempt to discredit him. 'Don't make our work seem so similar.'

'But it is similar,' the General cried. 'And you know it. My guns have a music as they try to smash the defences of your half of the world. Your music also tries to smash its way into dull brains, to disseminate what you call beauty and civilization. Doesn't it? Why don't you do a really great action, and admit it?'

'I don't need to,' Evart said.

'We're both fighters, drumming our troops into battle at opposite poles, both trying to conquer the world in our different ways. And because our ways are different and our music such great distances apart, one of us must go.'

'Us, of course,' Evart said, unable to contest the General's definition of total war.

'Don't jump to conclusions. You aren't dead yet.'

'And neither are you.'

With a smile the General said: 'Why don't you add that

extra word? Why not give in to the luxury of it – "And neither are you, *unfortunately*." There, I've said it for you!'

'Thank you,' Evart said, nearer than ever before to seeing the truth in the General's words.

'But you won't play now for a long time.'

This was not replied to. Evart looked beyond him, through the window at rolling white clouds over distant hills that sent out their eternal noises of bombardment, sounds that had become as natural as once were the bird songs performed among its trees.

'Did you volunteer to entertain your troops?'

He's trying to catch me out, Evart thought. He wants to trick me into admitting that I love the thing he loves. He said casually: 'One day I received a letter from the War Minister requesting that we play to the troops, which meant, as far as anything can mean, that I volunteered.' He spoke contemptuously now: 'One week we're free, and the next we're here as prisoners.'

'Well, don't take it so badly,' the General said smoothly.

'The orchestra as a whole will take it very badly, naturally. And they have reason to, of course.'

The General looked at him sardonically. 'You're lucky to be prisoners. It's a sheer accident that you're sitting here now, because by all the rules of this war you should have been massacred by the train. But to capture a symphony orchestra in war is a very rare thing indeed, so I must do what I can for you, in the interests of culture.' He unconsciously laid his hand on the casualty lists and stood up, pushing back his chair, listening for a few moments to gunfire coming from another sector in the north. 'Though whether there'll be any culture left when this war's over, I don't know.'

Evart looked across at him. 'Neither do I,' he said. 'Which is the only confession I have, one that I don't suppose will help my orchestra to stay alive and go on playing.'

The General lost patience with his prisoner: 'Is that all you have to say then? Don't you know that I shouldn't be talking to you now? You suspect me of trying to get a confession out of you, which is ridiculous, because you've nothing to tell me of any value, and nothing to confess. To us you're no more than a piece of wood for a winter fire. You should be dead, together with your whole orchestra, and you have nothing to say against this fact, no protest to make, no plan to try and save yourself. To me it seems that you aren't alive any more, that we've captured a dead man, which may have been one of the reasons that contributed to your not being killed by my soldiers – they knew you were already dead and so felt no need to kill you.'

Evart did not bother to break in and remind him that the soldiers *had* tried to kill them. Perhaps the General's right though, he thought, in saying I'm dead, since I don't contradict him even when I know he's wrong. He was still talking: 'Do you know what I'd be doing if I were in your place? I'd be telling the person I was speaking with about my nation, expounding my ideas as to why I was better than he, why I intended to stay alive as long as possible, why the ideas I had were the only ones worth having.'

'Would it make much difference if I did?' Evart demanded.

The General's smile gave a grim expression to his face: 'If I'd never had any faith up to now which side would win this war, but had just worked at the battles of it for my own diversion – in a dedicated way, of course – I'd know at this moment which side is the stronger and will come out on top.' He smiled again – with a feeling of having added the laurels of a dialectical victory to those of his physical accomplishments of the early morning.

'I didn't realize we'd been fighting a battle,' Evart said. 'In such a situation it's difficult to know where one stands. But if I fight at all it's often when I don't know I'm fighting. To me contests – or battles – aren't the sort you know all about. They're mystical and hidden things that I often don't realize are taking place at the time. For instance they might be movements within my consciousness, or in the air around my adversary's consciousness whom I haven't yet met; or hovering around other brains with the power to move – you or me, shall I say – in some way that neither of us suspect we'll move. Your surface battles decide nothing. They spill blood: that's all. The battles I'm talking about mean everything – in the end.'

Is there an end? wondered the General. 'They mean nothing,' he said, 'because there isn't an end.' His lack of a smile showed weariness – an indication that the interview was finished. He called Kondal, who had stood by, mute and vacant-eyed, an appendage strengthening the door. 'Take this gentleman back to the barn. See that he and his company are comfortable.'

The door closed. They marched away. He paced slowly towards the window behind his desk, then turned to the emotional poems of landscape pinned to the wall and stood looking at them, until they became a mirror through which he saw, beyond the merging of their beautiful colours, the mild fantasy of his half forgotten past.

He had strayed on to the dangerous ground of generalities. The régime wouldn't like that. The conversation had been merely stimulating, to the extent though that he took out a handkerchief to wipe the perspiration from neck and forehead.

A symphony orchestra complete with instruments!

They were prisoners, and he did not know what to do with them. By High Command Orders they should have been killed several hours ago, though even High Command might not want them shot if they knew it was a symphony orchestra he had captured. Standing comfortably with legs apart and hands clasped at his back he looked at the map and traced the route that the orchestra had taken to the battlefront. The thick black line of the railway came through woods and over mountain ranges, their train orientated and set like a toy going west, the head of an insidious arrow creeping nearer to the hour of its capture, to when it finally made an incision into his daily life.

What shall I do with them? It was a light-hearted question, for at the base of his thoughts he knew there was nothing for him to decide. He would submit the problem to High Command. I've no wish to massacre a symphony orchestra unless I'm ordered directly to do so, he said to himself. The war won't end one hour sooner if I kill them, or one hour later if I don't. He walked back to his desk and sat down. Silence had descended on the afternoon. Someone closed a door quietly in another part of the house, and the subdued working of a typewriter came from the Administrative Section. There were no sounds of motor-traffic outside, or the marching and shouting of soldiers, and all guns had ceased firing, as if the world in which he lived were taking a few minutes' sleep from the debilitating process of war.

'A symphony orchestra complete with instruments.'

Gradually, quietly and as if from out of nowhere, a slender line of melody drifted into his mind from the far-away past. He sat bemused, like someone on the point of going to sleep when the mind is left to its quaint incomprehensible meetings with what was imagined to be dead and buried. At first he felt a faint dislike for the melody because the still conscious part of his mechanical mind could not give it a name. But it was endless, persistent, stirring in its beauty, and he sat with hands to his face pondering on the name of the great composer from whose heart it had come. He had heard the melody before: the climax sprang at him from a bygone age, and the beginning drifted into him again immediately, from the city in which he had listened to it and seen it performed. Was it Berlin, Vienna, Leipzig? He heard the conductor's baton tapping the edge of the rostrum, breaking the thick silence of five thousand people that filled a great hall. The music acquired a new tone, changed, became items in a piano recital ticked off on a white programme, one out of a hundred performances hovering in memory . . . he shook himself free, and stood up.

He wanted to hear a symphony again, but the instrument for performing one, that he now possessed, must be destroyed. In a sudden fever of hope and desire he wondered whether High Command would after all want the orchestra shot. Perhaps not, he smiled, with a sudden unmitigated feeling of happiness. But the fever abated. There was no hope. Symphony orchestras were no asset to the nation, and could not matter to him, for now he was a general with command of his own armies, a position in which he must not expose himself to any accusation of sympathy towards such things.

Freedom. The freedom to attain your own successes within a formulated pattern. The freedom to serve. The freedom to submit uncertain questions to those in authority above you. Your conscience was a god who stated but did not decide. The conductor of the orchestra talks so forcibly about freedom, but what does he really know of it? Danger: an invisible flag that flies when unprofessional thoughts begin to dominate your mind. High Command were unpredictable in their policies. It could be that they would need the orchestra for some purpose, thereby delaying either its destruction, or transfer to the back areas, or both, in which case he might be able to induce them to play for him.

No. Impossible. It was a mere thought, easily crushed within the unnatural silence of the house and village. The morning's battle and breakthrough, followed by the lightning advance, seemed to be losing their power of consolation, and the slight hope that by some remote circumstance the orchestra might be able to play returned only to leave him with a sense of disappointment, in whose bitter wake he heard the various sounds in a concert hall before the performance began: uneven noises of people talking who had just come in from the lamplit darkness and driving rain, decisions to be made regarding the number and position of certain seats, discussions over rustling programmes, all welded into a discreet excitement as the orchestra took its place on the platform.

He reached forward for a signal pad, tore off the top sheet – with the marks of the last firm pencilling clearly shown – and wrote:

'During the course of the morning's offensive a number of prisoners were taken. They were strictly noncombatant prisoners comprising the members of a symphony orchestra captured complete with instruments. They are ninety-three in number. The fact that they were taken was an accident and therefore unavoidable. From the post-battle interrogation I gathered that they were on the way to the front to entertain their troops with a series of concerts. Owing to the extraordinary nature of these prisoners I would like a decision on what is to happen to them.'

He signed it, and added a low mark of priority so that it would not be transmitted until the slack period during the night, thereby delaying a reply until he entered his office the following morning.

He rang the bell on his desk and an orderly entered.

'Take this to the signals section,' he said. A lack of noise made him feel alone. The absence of other people did not disturb him as long as they could be heard. Then he felt safe, but at this moment it seemed as if he had been left in the middle of a wilderness deserted by his entire army, derelict beside his greatest enemy, silence. 'The orchestra's fate is out of my hands,' he suddenly said aloud, reaching for the cigarette box. 'High Command will solve everything. There's nothing I can do.'

But the feeling of some deep inner disturbance would

not leave him. He leaned forward and gave several rapid turns to the handle of the field telephone.

'Yes, your excellency?'

'Artillery Divisional Headquarters.' He waited, hoping that the silence would end. A dog barked, and several soldiers were talking outside, but it was not enough. 'Is that Artillery Divisional Headquarters?' he said loudly.

'Yes, this . . .'

He cut off the voice. 'All available batteries north of 017314 to open fire on the left spur of the enemy positions. Priority: immediate.'

He repeated the message, slammed the receiver back on its base, stood up, tugged the creases from his tunic and, as the rhapsodic drumbeat of gunfire came in louder and louder on the wind, walked out of the room on his way to the staff meeting that was set for six o'clock.

6

Hardly anyone had spoken since the bombardment began. Howitzer flashes came from the foothills and were carried through cracks in the barn door to explode like blue lights of sickness before their eyes. The grumbling persistent narrative of the guns gnawed like half dead rodents at their guts, and even when the bombardment stopped no one spoke for a while, for the reason then that it was too silent and they drew fear from the suspicious emptiness left by the noise. Gradually the almost five-score men generated a sound of their own. Their hearts beat normally again because the danger had become only half felt, and they began to talk, and finally to move about, penetrating the obstacles of shadow dividing each group. Bender had discovered that there was fuel still in the storm lamps on the shelf, and stumblingly took them around. Their turned-up wicks, throwing out circles of yellow light, reflected bales of hay as box-like shadows on the walls, from whose rim arms of thinner shadow occasionally gesticulated.

Evart looked out of a barred window at the back of the barn, through a row of soil-caked bottles on its ledge, towards a black crest-line of hills that made an undulating demarcation between earth and sky, a sky almost blue from a full moon shining above the roof. A green signal rocket streaked up from the hills and went out just as it turned for the descent, like a lighted hand that had failed to reach the stars. Wind from the south-west carried an odour of smouldering fire, which made him shiver both at the strength of the breeze and the tale of destruction that it carried. Behind him men talked in low voices. Someone laughed. Others played cards at the makeshift table, and many read books or out-of-date newspapers. A vanguard of grey clouds came over the summit-line of the hills, covering the first constellation that sparkled above it and, unwilling to witness their disappearance, Evart turned and went back to the others.

Six lamps lit up a large space in the centre, and walking into it was like leaving the lonely darkness of a wood and entering the comfortable firelight of the tents. Several men were already sleeping, and he avoided outstretched legs and arms to reach the place where his coat was spread.

On hearing him sit down, Starnberg asked: 'Do you have a cigarette?'

He tossed a packet to him, then picked up a book that he felt no desire to open. Starnberg gave them back: 'I meant for yourself.'

Evart lit one, leaned contentedly, the match falling from his fingers while still alight. Its flame leaped along a piece of straw, apparently went out, then reached forward with a yellow hook to a more combustible heap of fuel. From the corner of his eye he saw it, dragged his overcoat over the flame and hammered it to death with his boots. 'We have to be careful,' he said. 'It's foolish to smoke with all this hay about.'

'What else can you do if you're feeling depressed?' Starnberg smiled easily, much of the anxiety out of his face since Evart had described his meeting with the General. Voices were heightened in the card game:

'I'll raise you two.'

'I'll see you.'

Laughter and the clapping of victorious hands, the rattle of collected coins. Evart looked into the complicated pattern made by individual straws of hay, and when there was nothing in sight by which he could gauge the proportion of their size, they seemed like the rafters of some fallen-in house-roof.

'Did you see anything interesting from the window?'

'A few stars,' Evart replied. 'Certainly not our victorious troops coming to get us out of this.' He turned to him. 'What were you thinking at dawn this morning? Did you imagine we'd be here?'

'I'm a timid man,' Starnberg replied. 'I always live through surprises before they come so that they won't come, especially unpleasant surprises. But this was totally unexpected, and when that happens, I call it God.'

'And leave it at that, I suppose?'

'No, just hope that things will improve again.'

'It is easy to see I'm depressed then?' Evart asked, sitting down once more.

'No, but I can sense it. The others think your silence is only calmness in face of a difficult situation. They think you're "setting an example".'

'Which you don't believe?' Evart smiled.

'Of course. Only I know how hard it is for you as well.' Shadows from the lamp rippled over Starnberg's face, and Evart steadied the flame by lowering the wick almost to nothing, then turning it up again. Here we are, he thought, two men consoling each other because we don't have courage. 'You know quite well,' he said, 'that I'm not setting an example. It's good that the others think I am, I suppose, but you know it's not true.'

Starnberg's grin became a subdued laugh. 'Whose turn to deal?' came from the card game.

'Not yours.'

'I hope I'm lucky this round.'

'Not a third time.'

'Wait and see.'

'Royal flush for me.'

'Before you came on this trip something put you into the right frame of mind for what's happening' – he eased himself from his cramped position and stretched his legs out over the straw – 'so I wonder whether you'd have set

70

the same "example" if you'd been in a normal state of mind?'

'What makes you think I'm caught up in any trouble?'

'I guessed it.'

'How?'

'I don't know. Everything seems more real here, and so it's easier to sense things. It's like sometimes when you see buildings at dusk: their walls and windows shine and glitter with an exaggerated light and things stand out more clearly than at other times. You see what I mean? I feel, you see, that values have altered since this morning. The air we breathe has been changed by what we've gone through.' He peered for a moment beyond the range of his own lamp, at other groups more subdued now, talking quietly like classes in a school of conspiracy. The flames in some lamps were less steady, and their shadows waved undisciplined on the walls. Those playing cards were losing interest, did not make so much noise, and between each game they lapsed into desultory conversation; those who had stretched out and gone to sleep had done so with lamps still shining. He turned back to Evart. 'Why don't you tell me what's on your mind?'

'There's nothing to tell.'

'It helps a great deal to talk to people. We can still speak to each other; they can't rob us of that,' Starnberg said, though with a note of sadness in his voice.

'They could cut our tongues out,' Evart said, unwilling to go far into the discussion.

'Propaganda,' Starnberg retorted.

'And cut our hands off so that we wouldn't be able to write or make signs like deaf-and-dumb men.' He separated the hay with his fingers and stubbed a cigarette ruthlessly against the earthen floor beneath.

'They could even kill us,' Starnberg laughed.

'This talk is like your walls and windows at dusk,' Evart said with some sarcasm. 'There's no reality about it.'

71

Starnberg was piqued. 'If you want realism, talk some yourself.'

'All right, I will. Tell me how this sounds: if we could somehow make a rush from the barn, all of us, into the darkness, how many of us do you think would finally get back over those hills?'

'We're too well guarded,' Starnberg said. 'And the hills are too far away.'

'No they're not. I looked at them through the window for a full hour. Nor too high either. And the terrain between us and the hills isn't as flat as we thought it was. There are woods, streams, hollows, plenty of places to hide. A few of us would get back.'

'What good would that be? Stick to the principle: if six escape we'd still be destroyed.'

'That's your view, from behind your shine and glitter.'

'It's yours too, and you know it,' Starnberg exclaimed, angered at last.

'I wish I did know it,' Evart said with regret. 'That's the trouble: I don't know whether it's worthwhile trying to smash our way out of here or not.'

'You've lost the habit of action,' Starnberg reminded him.

'I could soon pick it up,' he cried hastily, as if he had been accused of some petty crime, 'if it were worth it. And I'm beginning to think that even if only three of us got back it would be of some value.'

'I still don't think you should try.'

'I wish to God I could. But I could no more pick up a gun than I could pick up a poisonous snake, and you know it.'

'Neither could I.'

'Not even in self-defence. It's a handicap nowadays, like being blind and lame. It always has been a handicap, I suppose, and always will be for us.'

'For us, yes,' Starnberg agreed, 'but not for people like

the General. That's why we're trapped in this barn like animals, because somebody has glorified war as a way of solving problems or testing theories. It's too strong for us to fight against, it seems, except by using their own methods.'

Evart could not see through the livid façade of Starnberg's words: each one by itself was tangible, strung together they made some sort of sense even, but the meaning of that sense was irrelevant. Hoping – but failing – to give them meaning, he looked around the barn, at the card game that had gathered new life. 'Come on,' one impatient player called out, 'throw in!'

'Don't you think we'd better deal first?' The crackle of shuffling cards came to him, and laughter. He saw neither answer nor consolation.

'How can they be so completely engrossed?'

'Because they're glad of a rest,' Starnberg answered. 'It's good to be thrown into a vacuum after weeks of hard work. Most of them can relax at last.'

'We're among the few who can't,' Evart remarked. 'What's *your* reason, Starnberg?'

'I've lost the art of it,' he said quickly. 'I can't just stretch myself out on the straw and think about nothing. I wish I could.'

'That's because you're worried about what's going to happen. I wonder if they'd be so relaxed if they realized what might be in store for us?'

'Perhaps. At the moment they're prisoners, and that's all they're really aware of.' He loosened the top button of his shirt that had suddenly become too tight at the neck. 'They only know what's happening at the moment, and therefore know the truth.'

'And we who have ideas about what's going to happen don't know the truth?' Evart asked, a question set mainly for himself.

'Only prophets think about the future,' Starnberg said,

adding as an afterthought: 'The wide, distant future, I mean, not whether they'll have food tomorrow.'

'But if the future's false, then they must be fools,' Evart retorted.

'No. Sometimes their prophecies come true, otherwise they wouldn't be prophets! Look at the others,' he went on eagerly, waving his arms towards them. 'They're either asleep, reading or playing cards. They're living in their little worlds of truth. If we tried to tell them the truth of this situation according to us, most of them wouldn't believe it, and a few at least would be killed trying to escape. As it is they seem to be guarded from this so-called truth by some sort of natural protection, an immunity that I hope will save them, and therefore myself. What you think is the truth may turn out to be something quite different.'

A gang of soldiers were passing outside, some singing loudly in high jangling uncouth notes that nevertheless suggested an air of gaiety. They paused in their march. There was a scuffle and tap of boots, a clapping of hands to a rapid impromptu dance that ended only by the heavy breathing of exhausted men, a sound heard for a second between the final decisive step and the spectators' applause. They passed on, and as their noise diminished a solitary rifle-shot came from the edge of the village. Some of the sleepers in the barn were disturbed, and a few grunts sounded as they turned over in their dreams. Evart nodded towards the receding soldiers: 'That's all the truth there is. That, and these men losing their sleep while it passes.'

Starnberg looked away, hiding a mask of discouragement. 'It's not true,' he said. 'I refuse to believe it.' His steadily piled argument in favour of a future existing for them had collapsed beneath the sound of a gang of drunken soldiers passing the barn. He wanted to resume the discussion and half turned to argue his case back into shape, but his words would not conjoin, lost their focus. He could

74

not begin to speak. Was this anguish present because he was unable to explain what he felt, or was it because he thought he may be going to die soon? he wondered, as he unfolded his sleeping-bag, flattened a heap of straw, then rolled up his overcoat for a pillow, working with slow and tired movements.

Evart moved into a better sitting position, hands clasped behind his head. 'The others understand the situation just as well as we do, and know exactly what to expect from the Gorsheks. I'm sure they have as much courage as us.'

'All right. I'm only trying to justify my own fears,' Starnberg said, pausing in his work. 'And also, of course, the fear that you feel also.'

'I wish I did feel it,' Evart said.

'Of course you feel it,' Starnberg retorted hotly. 'It may have been numbed by something, but it's there just the same.'

'It obviously must be,' Evart admitted. 'I'm not trying to hide my feelings. If a man has nothing to live for, that doesn't mean he wants to die. Somebody who's in pain doesn't want to die to get rid of his pain, but only to throw it off.' His eyes were burning with fatigue, but he continued: 'A prophet may be a fool, but if he is martyred for his foolishness he at least dies in hope, which we won't be able to do. That's one reason why I feel a numbness: if we die we die in despair, and I don't want to die like that.' He enjoyed the ease that talking gave, and went on: 'I've spent most of this trip thinking about my wife.'

'That's not unusual; so have I.'

'Yes, but I found out not long ago that she'd been having an affair. I suppose it's ludicrous to brood over such a thing, but I can't help it. I've been comparing it to the situation we're in now.'

'There is no comparison,' Starnberg objected.

'Not to you maybe. But to me it's a jump from a narrow personal trap to a wider problem. Three of us only were involved in the first: this one concerns everybody in the world, though only a few people realize it. My little tragedy – which it was, and still seems – happens every day; this can occur only once. One was a little death, in me; this is a big death, in everybody. The little one I never expected; this one I've always dreaded. I'm not afraid for myself, for my own skin, I tell you – only for the orchestra as a unit.' He looked up, saw that Starnberg knew he had not yet finished: 'We were only taken prisoner today,' he went on, 'but you think a lot in a few hours. One thought is hope and the one that comes after it is despair. When they meet they give a true picture. The best thing to do is think as little as you can, though I suppose if one's given to thinking there's not much you can do about it. Maybe if you think long enough it leads you around to seeing more reason for hope, though at the moment I doubt it.'

His hands shook, and he found it difficult to light a cigarette. Nearly everyone in the barn was asleep, and he stood up, steadying himself by a bale of hay. Some of the lamps had gone out for lack of oil, and shadows on the walls became indistinct. He returned to the window at the back of the barn, looked between its bars at the cloud-gaps in the sky, where moonlight and stars levered a moment of hope into his heart. Muffled firing came from the north, and a few shouts echoed through the wrecked village. The distance into the heavens doubled and redoubled the longer he looked, until it forced him to turn his eyes away. He hoped that the clouds would completely cover the sky and obliterate the blue gaps, and he lowered his head to ground-level as if to give this time to take place, but when he saw the sky again many more clouds had moved away, and vast areas of light-blue shone with patterns of stars. The sight of them did not give him hope. The first time he had read as a boy that the nearest star was twenty-seven million miles away from the earth he had gazed at the stars and pondered on this terrible distance, dwelt on the pure beauty of their mute, shining inaccessibility until he wept, and now he felt similar pangs because it was possible that the inspired sensation he felt on seeing them was about to be taken away, from him and from the others. There were many problems, infinitely distant and complicated, that could not be explained.

He stood until his body ached with exhaustion, then walked back towards his sleeping space. Only one lamp burned, but its light was enough to show him the way to where he had left his coat.

7

All military operations were monotonously similar, and all losses proportionate to the value of ground gained. For the first time this so far unformulated principle of Gorshek tactics, which the General had unconsciously fought with all his imaginative powers to prove untrue, came home to him as a fact that no amount of dialectics could gainsay. He experienced this new pain of unbiased vision while reading a long despatch regarding troop and ammunition reserves for the next offensive, and the sudden disturbance of a knock that came at the door made a welcome break in his chain of ideas, and subordinated his mind once more to duty.

'Come in,' he shouted.

'A signal, your excellency.'

He watched the orderly go out, then rested his eyes on the blank panels of the closed door. Duty was sidestepped by his too inquisitive brain, which went on to tell him that if a War-god existed he was a shrivelled parsimonious chemist whose scales were always evenly balanced, with blood on one side and soil on the other. If you were lucky enough to advance a few miles at little cost you could be sure of having the bad luck of retreat later; or to push on another short mile only after a blood-bath that equated the chemist's scales with the price of the first advance. For in this war courage had long since been brought to such a pitch, tenacity to such fine limits of stress, logistics and the reading of each other's minds to such perfection, that decisive victory was hardly possible. Up to the time of the General's advance the two armies had faced each other and never moved beyond a twenty-mile corridor of soil in which their ribbon defence lines had swayed back and forth for years, though during that time both had suffered losses as if a dozen major battles had been fought and lost in equal proportion. The General realized that unless he accumulated sufficient material – human and mechanical – to break over the mountain range in the spring, the line would once more solidify, and the Gorsheks would find themselves in such a continually exposed position on the lower terrain that sooner or later their whole line would break and his nation would be driven to death in the northern ice forests or the bleak waters of the great western ocean. If his spring offensive were successful, however (and he was still extremely confident that it would be), a similar fate would lie in store for the enemy. One way or another, the War-god holding his nicely balanced scales would be smashed to the ground.

The picture of the Gorshek hero hanging nearby pulled his line of vision on to it, as if for some time it had been trying to catch his attention in order to caution him against the machinations of his too fertile mind. The General suddenly felt that he had seen the face before, though he could not decide when and where because he knew neither the name of the man whom the portrait was supposed to represent, nor the date of his death (if he had died at all, which he doubted, for it seemed now that he had seen him quite recently). It was not a disagreeable face, with grey expressive eyes, firm jaw, well-set mouth and nose, and a hardly perceptible smile that could have been as much the first sign of epileptic rage as of genuine humour, and the General tried to read into its features the contents of the signal just brought in by the orderly. But no answer was writ large there, for it was a face capable of indicating profound depths behind a façade that appeared blank, or of concealing a blank mind while engineering its façade to appear profound. So the General looked down and scanned the block capitals written on thin paper:

79

He had not slept well, having been too much concerned with the fate of the orchestra, caught all night by a fluctuating hope that it would not have to be destroyed, and that if he received a favourable signal from High Command he could perhaps persuade the orchestra to give at least one concert in the barn before they were moved to whatever area was specified. There was no denying the power of the flimsy signal before him, and he inwardly regretted the order even more because he knew High Command's trick of reaching decisions. They had in no way considered his problem, of that he was certain. State rules and policy were so rigidly enforced in order to keep the nation secure that a manual of government had been built into an electronic brain and, no matter how simple were the problems to be solved and decisions to be made, all queries were thrust into it, and later verified by respective ministers. Each department had its separate Brain – War, Food, Munitions – competent and trustworthy servants of the régime that never failed in loyal interpretation. Correct answers in state examinations were checked by the Brains, and those papers that did not tally with their delicate mechanisms were spewed out in shreds. With this in mind the General looked again at the signal: a hallmark of Brain precision, and High Command sanction. Immediately. Marshal-in-Chief.

He gripped the edge of the desk, his heart beating fast with anger. The signal had come too suddenly, though it could not have come any other way. He sat with fingers across his heavy chin, the consolation of his recent victory having left his mind filled only with reasons why he would not now be able to hear a symphony played by the prisoners in the barn. A pervading sense of frustration was sided against him, blocking off all solutions that might have helped him had his problem been of a military nature. I was a fool to hope, he told himself, for hope makes one suffer; should therefore be controlled and eradicated. Hope that is smashed is probably the basis of all suffering, and was one of those prime unrealistic qualities that set you at emotional loggerheads with High Command for ordering the deaths of people you would rather not kill, which was a stupid situation in which to find yourself, he thought. One moment he hoped something might still occur to save the orchestra, and at the next he regretted that the orchestra had been taken prisoner, and cursed Kondal.

This slow deadlock gave way to a deep sense of discipline, ingrained during endless years with the Army. He was, he found it necessary to remind himself, a soldier above all else, someone who must obey orders as well as give them, and if High Command said the orchestra were to be killed then there was nothing else he could do but see that they were killed. He must not permit shallow and sentimental feelings to interfere with duty, must stifle regret, stop hope reaching him, and dismiss his anger as futile and childish.

He remembered the stark fate of those who did not obey orders. They were tried before courts that, though staffed with human judges, gave out verdicts issued first by a jurisprudent Brain. Sentences were rigid for such crimes: offenders were relegated to convict category, had their epaulettes and uniform changed for a sackcloth costume of even worse quality than that worn by his soldiers, were then armed with a spade and sent in open trucks on a one-way ticket to endless exile in some nether corner of the continent, never to be heard of again. They were not even killed. The term of sentence was known by a special verb: to be levelled. Levelled with what? he had wondered. Levelled, he gathered, with the animals of the earth, chained out in the wilderness at the mercy of infinitely fickle seasons; heat, cold, starvation and the whiplash of enforced labour. Apart from conscience, there were many reasons why one must obey orders.

He took up a pen to check details of ammunition stocks, but his mind was disturbed by half secret melodies coming from nowhere, wandering up as softly as plumed smoke, playing themselves one into another until they grew louder and more insistent; and he jerked his head to dislodge them as if he were trying to shake off a fly. Resistance was fatal, for the music came stronger than ever, breaking through tunes of marches and folk-songs, snapping strong bonds of Nation and Progress, Survival and War, until his brain was swimming with a sensation of peace and calmness that up to that moment he thought he had never known.

He rang a bell, and the door opened. Kondal stood before him. 'Yes, your excellency?'

'Take two guards and fetch the conductor of the orchestra.'

He waited for the door to close, as if his thoughts would be detected should they stray outside to the corridor. A rift was growing in him, and he hardly knew how it came to be there. It was like a poisonous plant that sprouts up in the night out of clean soil, totally unexpected, and was dividing him between duty and some new emotion that made him afraid. He reasoned, regardless of any reason to which he had ever been accustomed, that High Command had no soul to order the deaths of ninety-three musicians, that there could be no purpose in it, and that it was utterly unnecessary. He asked himself what could be done, and from meditating on various means of action he looked guardedly to where guns rumbled only a few miles away, where a discreet sort of freedom still existed; but the line dividing him from that part of the world was so strong that he had difficulty in breaking it down even in thought.

He stood by the window and saw the conductor of the orchestra coming from the barn, between two guards,

Kondal marching in front. Soldiers stared at them as they crossed the open space before the house, and the General himself watched until they ascended the steps and were cut from sight. I suppose they must be shot if High Command say so, he argued with himself, but if I could find sufficient excuse to soften their order and let the orchestra give concerts to myself and other officers, I would do so. He picked up the signal again, hoping that the words would have altered since last looking at it: to be shot immediately; signed; nothing else.

Disappointment made him unexpectedly bitter. Failure to capture a hill, a wood, to secure a river crossing, was accepted with good grace, a shrug of the shoulders, an hour of regret perhaps for a plan gone haywire and a few moments' calculation on how to reinforce his weakened line, but because High Command issued an order which he had in any case expected, the emotion that had formerly made his reason more deadly in the art of war now threatened to drive him to foolish actions which would be dangerous.

He recalled Evart's tall thin figure striding between his guards, a clear memory indicating that the struggle had not yet begun. The one wise thing to do, he knew, throwing the signal back into the tray, was kill as soon as possible, thereby foiling the destructive forays of hope and suffering that came against him. He waited eagerly for a knock on the door, and when it came he was so startled that several seconds passed before he could reply to it. He told Kondal and the guards to wait outside, and the door closed behind Evart.

The General took the signal from the tray, looked at it as if it were a long and complicated document that he could not understand.

Evart remained standing, saw sunlight falling in a beam across a blotting pad on the General's desk, and noticed a tiny red pimple coming to a head on the General's forehead as he bent over the paper. Looking around the room he saw a lizard twist swiftly up the wall, run across a delta on one of the maps, cross a corner and disappear behind the Gorshek portrait near the door. He turned to see the General looking at him, blowing smoke from a freshly lit cigarette. 'I hope you're being well looked after?'

Evart gave a formal answer: 'We've nothing to complain of, though we'd naturally like to know what's going to happen to us.'

'I'm interested in your future too,' the General smiled, observing the anxiety that his prisoner tried so hard to hide. He picked up the signal. 'Who is second in command of your orchestra?'

Evart was suspicious. 'A man called Starnberg.'

The General wrote the name down on a pad and threw the pencil aside with a clatter. He saw the puzzled look still on his prisoner's face, but rather than explain his question asked nonchalantly: 'Did your company sleep well in the barn last night?'

'Between bombardments.'

'Bombardments? There were no bombardments. A few shells were fired in the north perhaps. We're conserving ammunition for the spring offensive.'

Evart was irritated and disturbed by the quizzical attitude of his opponent. 'Now you seem to be giving *me* military information.'

'Perhaps. But you won't be able to use it. That's the difference.'

'What if I escape?'

The General stood up, leaned forward so that his face was nearer to Evart. 'Anyone trying to escape,' he said angrily, 'will be shot down by my guards. No one will succeed in getting away.'

'They may. My men are speaking of it.'

'Your men are not speaking of it, or you wouldn't have told me. In any case, there won't be any guard after

84

tomorrow morning.' He sat down again and leaned back in his chair. (The rims of Evart's eyes contracted at the sound of this implication. So that's why I'm here, he thought. But he hoped his conclusion was a false one. Trick number two: to break a man down. Perhaps that was what he wanted. He held his hands behind his back, waiting for the General to speak again.) He picked up, put down, folded the paper on which the signal was written, as if suddenly afraid of what it said, visibly hesitating several times before speaking. 'You see,' he announced in a voice of unbiased authority, 'I have some bad news.' He knew he need not have said more, but did so because a verbal repetition of High Command's order would strengthen his own resolution to obey it. 'You and your entire company are to be shot tomorrow morning.'

There was a long pause. Evart was drained white by this more predatory vampire of the expected; bleached, in spite of all fine theories regarding what it meant, by the fearful thought of common simple death – like something he had been circling at a distance for years, and then to be suddenly thrust close to see with horror the emptiness it held in.

Yet by firm control he fought off what primeval feelings threatened, drew his spirit back from the burning ice; and presented the outward calm appearance of staring hard at the General. 'We aren't soldiers,' he said at last. 'We didn't come to the front to fight.'

'I know,' the General said, 'but that's not the point. The Gorshek High Command have given the order to me. I can do nothing about it. There's nothing else to say or discuss, because their decision is final.'

'Can't you question it? You don't order a symphony orchestra to be destroyed. It's impossible.'

He was weary, already felt as though he had done a whole day's work. 'The Gorshek High Command do not normally take prisoners,' he said, as if reading from a book of instructions, 'and your deaths are ordered because it would cost food, time, labour and anxiety to guard you. We've no use for a symphony orchestra, and we don't want to waste good men guarding you, when they can be better employed fighting. That's their idea in ordering you to be shot. That's what they call logic. And I can find no better name for it.'

Evart came forward and leaned over his desk. 'They don't know what they're doing,' he cried. 'Even your nation must know it's a terrible crime to kill us, that there's no reason or justice in it.' He looked behind at the closed door, at the maps on either side, then turned back to see the General, still sitting behind his desk, lift the small bell and shake it, and heard its sound: like drops of water sprinkling the stultified atmosphere in the room.

'I'm sorry,' he said, replacing the bell, turning up the fingers of a pair of white gloves behind him. 'But there's nothing I can do.' The door had already opened, and Kondal waited.

'Would you help us if you could?'

'What do you think?' the General said, but Evart had walked to where his guards were standing. He turned however to say with infuriated irony: 'None of us will be given time, it seems, to solve such a huge problem.'

'While you're alive you can always hope for time.'

'Not when you've already been condemned,' Evart retorted.

'Then I'm sorry for you,' the General said soberly. 'I pity you in all sincerity because you can't understand our way of life, and never will be able to understand it. You see, in the historic progress of the world we, the Gorsheks, are carrying on the torch of suffering, of death, of danger and birth. In our nation, by the very pattern of its autocratic existence, we foster rebellion, but we always crush it. That's the secret of our internal strength, something of which perhaps you've never heard or understood.

It's only in this way that we keep history and human nature going at the same time. A feat in the universe. For those Gorsheks that don't rebel we promise the best life within our power. This promise is easy to keep because our past failures have been so great (as you know, we've had such catastrophic famines) that they expect very little. The ambitions of their tight stomachs have become so modest that we can almost meet them. Think of that! You, on your side, will never be able to keep your rash promises, especially while our nation goes on bleeding you white. And our nation will always exist. I say it without boasting.'

But Evart detected boasting in his voice. He made one last effort on behalf of the orchestra. 'So there's nothing I can offer you in exchange for not destroying us? For instance, what about accepting my life in place of the others?'

'I was expecting you to say that. Being a weak man, what else could you offer but your own life? No, you'll have to come up with a better bargain than that. Your life is no good to me. All I have to do is lift my little finger and you'd be riddled with bullets, a piece of meat for the dogs to feed on. Offer me something valuable,' he laughed.

Evart thought: He's insane. 'You're the Devil,' he said, 'and want my soul.'

He laughed again, loudly and genuinely. 'Soul! What a strange vocabulary you have. That word's been rubbed out of our dictionaries for years.'

'Why don't you kill us now, and be done with it?' Argument seemed finished: more would only increase the General's cat-and-mouse satisfaction. Yet argument still seemed the only hope.

'Do you think I'm a humanitarian?' the General was saying. 'Well I'm not. I'm a soldier. But because I admit I'm not a humanitarian I suppose you think I'm not a human being? You imagine I'm a robot, a man without a heart, an automaton that moves when it's wound up and refuelled. You may be right, but if you are then you must say it about everyone else in the world. You think I'm a robot because High Command has only to get its wireless operators to press a morse key and I'm set in motion. You think that, don't you? Well, you're wrong. Only God moves me.'

'I hope so.'

'You hope so?' he laughed. 'Well don't delude yourself into thinking that my God is the same as yours and that I'm going to lose my life by letting you go free. I'm not. I'm sure you'd accept it if I did, because you're just as militaristic as I am, only I'm a million times better man than you are.'

'By whose standards?' Evart demanded.

'Mine. At the moment mine are the only ones that count.'

'At the moment perhaps. But as each moment passes another moment leapfrogs over it into the future. Hasn't that ever occurred to you? There's a great future in store for those that think about eternity, and you aren't one of them.' Evart, all through this duo-rocketing, felt uneasily as if his words were submarined harmonics of some higher meaning: but this higher meaning was so remote above the twin-reaching of each opposite soul that he had to be content with what form the proof of its existence took, to be satisfied that it was possible for him to dimly perceive it at all.

The General smiled. 'Who's to be the judge of that?'

'I am. That's *my* prerogative and luxury. You've just condemned us, and now you'd like to judge us as well. You can't have it both ways.'

'I don't want it both ways. The thing is that it doesn't matter a great deal to me whether you're killed or not. If you want to know the truth, it's this: if I had my way I'd let you go. But High Command say I'm to kill you. I'm not heartless. But I'm not a fool either. I know whose side

I'm on. That's my strength, that I admit I'm on a side. Your weakness is that you won't ally yourself to a side.'

'And I never shall. At least not the despicable sides that are offered me. There must be something better than those two. Perhaps your atrocity of killing us will be proof of this better side, the third way, that you and your nation can't know anything about and therefore ever control.'

'For myself,' the General said, 'I'd get no comfort from speculations like that. But I hope it's as useful and helpful to you as it sounds, though I doubt it.'

Evart, unable to find an answer, turned to leave.

'There's one more thing I have to say,' the General called to him. 'You can tell your orchestra that if they play a symphony for myself and some other officers in the barn tomorrow night, I'll postpone their execution for two days.'

A sudden renewed lustre came back into Evart's eyes. Amusement and astonishment were a part of it, but also it was lit by hope, lifting him completely out of his dazed resignation. 'Why are you playing with us?' he asked.

'I'm not playing any game at all. I want to hear a symphony, and this is the only way I can do it.'

'But if you can put our execution off for two days, you can set us free.'

'Impossible,' the General said, with such emphasis that Evart detected the lack of conviction.

'I don't believe it. You've only to call off your guards and let us walk out of the barn.' He looked into the General's eyes, trying to pin down the thoughts mirrored there until he recognized the direction they were taking. The General turned away, angry at his sudden feeling of shame.

'I've put the proposition to you,' he said. 'If you don't want to accept it, say so. But remember that the others may have different ideas.' His stern tone broke the temporary contact between them.

Evart stood away from the desk. 'I'll see what they say.'

The General looked across at Kondal who waited for orders. 'Take him back to the barn.' Evart did not seem to notice the curt tap on his back from Kondal, but automatically moved towards the door. He placed himself between his guards with unconscious accuracy and, followed by Kondal, walked off down the corridor.

The General had leapt, and he could not whirl himself back to the top of the cliff. He had made his request to the orchestra and given them terms, and the gulf dividing him from his sense of discipline had widened still more. Thinking these things, he suddenly saw a possibility – out of what the orchestra would think was pride and what he would know as stupidity – of them not accepting his offer.

All background noises died away from his mind. He no longer noticed the guns, the soldiers and other noises of war outside his window. Even the map-covered walls had folded up their influence and retreated out of his thought's range. A fly that settled on the black hairs of his wrist ascended into the air again in disgust when it did not have the pleasure of being disturbed by an irate other hand. He looked at the blank space before him on his desk, as if seeing a symphony orchestra performing in its central vacant space, staring at it until the wood gave out sounds of music. When it is all over, he thought at the end of an imaginary movement, I'll wonder how I spent my time deciding such a difficult question, and how I came to carry out such an impossible order.

He was lulled into areas where thought was unquestioned, forgetting what penalties were paid for decisions that came from such a state. Symphonies were played before him, and he was one of a numberless audience receiving the impact of their splendid sound. His memory held back none of all the tunes he had ever heard, and he remembered so many that he began to discriminate between what he wanted to hear and what could wait for another time, feeling the joy of the multitude as they listened with him, and the inspiration of the orchestra as they played. The multitude swelled, and the orchestra grew in sound and numbers until everyone in the universe could hear it. One moment the music was titanic, then it was subdued by a downward crest until it could hardly be heard, though people were listening for it right to the ends of space.

A slight feather of distraction must somehow have crept into a corner of his mind, for the multitudes began to fall off like leaves melting from a tree, and the invisible wands of music did not describe such a vast circle. Magically and gradually its influence decreased, until he saw again the television-like panel on his desk, and fear threatened to push the last traces of music from him. Disturbing thoughts of guilt returned, souring his mind of music until he looked up and saw the walls around him covered with maps. A fly alighted again on his hand. He watched it, gave it time to settle, and suddenly brought his other hand down on it quicker than the strike of a snake. He rolled it on to the floor, and felt disappointment when the pain of his doubts began creeping back into him after a few moments when he had felt nothing but the beautiful and empty action of killing a fly. Painlessly now the fly lay on the floor, and he savoured its emptiness and compared it with his own stagnation of a problem, where all his pensive circumlocution had led him only to a stopgap decision.

Unrealistic of them to refuse my offer, he said to himself. Opening a desk-drawer below his knee, he drew out a large-scale map of the latest forward positions, looked at it intently for some minutes, then passed his thumb lightly along black-lined roads curving up the close orange contour-lines of the hill slopes. He pencil-marked around houses to be turned into forts, and when he came to a village examined its street formation with a magnifying glass. I'll get the cartographers to enlarge that area four times, he told himself, and fill in details by reconnaissance. On other maps he picked out defence positions, then studied sectors overlapping his own, forgetting for some time the problem that seemed to have been bothering him ever since he was born, making notes and sketches on a pad by his elbow, tearing off several sheets and fastening them together with a paper clip.

How long will I have to wait for their reply? he wondered, pressing the pencil against his chin. He looked at his watch: half an hour to lunch. Went back to his maps. An orderly came in with a sheaf of signals, and he read each one slowly, making notes from some on the margin of the map, throwing others aside into one of the trays. Deep echoes of gunfire rolled from the hills and, standing by the window, he saw varying shapes of smoke drifting skywards. Then the guns were silent, smoke dispersed, leaving nothing but warm blue sky above the hills. He rolled up the maps and put them back in the drawer, then separated important signals for action later in the day. The exhausting hours of the morning had left him weary, and he decided upon an hour's sleep after lunch. Wearing cap and gloves he walked to the door leading into his apartment and, when about to turn the knob, a knock came from the other door that gave on to the corridor.

Kondal had a message for him. 'From the prisoners in the barn, your excellency.'

The General took it without haste, stood by his desk, opened the paper and read it. He smiled at what he saw:

'My orchestra will play Tchaikovsky's Sixth Symphony (The Pathétique) for you in the barn at half past seven tomorrow night.'

8

The metal and leather of rusting horse harness, separated with penkives and used against the hardest brick, quickly buckled into uselessness. Starnberg, from where he was sitting, then watched the would-be escapers take two more hours to cut loose a depth of board and scrape away stone and rubble with bare hands.

Before Evart's visit to the General's office, escape had been mentioned but not seriously discussed, for it was imagined then that they had only to wait for the reappearance of their own soldiers to be set free; at the worst to undergo a year or so of captivity before the war was won. But Evart's news had altered this attitude and, led by Armgardson, a group of incensed violinists goaded their hands to a frenzy of work, tearing, burrowing, removing cement and stones in quiet and secrecy until, by the middle of the afternoon, it was possible for a man to squeeze through and look out at the fields, and to wriggle back in triumph grasping a handful of fresh soil whose smell suggested the growth of indomitable plants as well as the decaying mould that encompassed their death – with all the spirit of natural action lying between these two states.

Most of the orchestra were apathetic and would take neither risk nor trouble in trying to get away, while those who did want to escape became so fanatical in their desire that they would not wait for darkness, and refused to heed Starnberg's good sense that told them to do so. They turned each reason for making a daylight escape into the soundest common sense as far as they themselves were concerned: since no one would expect them to try in daylight the element of surprise would be on their side;

how could they find their way through unknown country at night? Daylight was the time, for they could orientate themselves before darkness fell. The sooner they got out of the barn the better, for who knew that the General would not kill them in an hour, within five minutes even, despite his wish to hear a symphony? In any case they weren't so well guarded now as they had been. And hadn't anyone noticed, for instance, that there were always more guards around during the night? The time was now, they insisted blindly, and Starnberg, after hearing them become more and more convinced at the sound of their own argument, withdrew from the loud voices of their planning.

Evart preferred to see nothing of what was happening, though Starnberg tried to break this strong façade. 'You shouldn't let them do it,' he said. 'It'll make things bad for the rest of us. They'll all be captured.'

'Perhaps, but what can the General do if they get caught? Shoot them? Well, that's what's going to happen anyway.'

'How do you know it is?' Starnberg cried. 'They might get killed trying to escape, and if the rest of us are set free later they'll have died for nothing.'

'I don't think so,' Evart said with finality. 'If they want to take their chance now, let them.'

Starnberg made one more attempt. 'Can't you at least persuade them to try this evening, when it's dark?'

'They know what they're doing,' Evart said.

The gap in the wall grew wider. Out of it lay an open field of unharvested beets, with semi-cultivated country beyond showing occasional clumps of stunted trees. A hundred yards from the barn was a dry ditch, and it was arranged that the violinists would crawl out to this, lie still in it until all was clear, then work their way slowly towards the hills.

Evart stood at the barred window to watch them go. There had been little disturbance from guns in the last few hours and he was glad of it. The General is keeping the world quiet for our concert, he surmised. Yet the silence was sinister; if the air were ablaze with shellfire they would have more chance of getting away, he reasoned, seeing the two white-faced violinists crawling through the narrow jagged gap.

He was absorbed in the mechanics of their escape, mentally rehearsing the system they had worked out, finding it faulty now only in the luck they did not have – of a wild bombardment to make a protective tunnel over them. The world was too silent for so rash a venture, as he had already explained – like rain which often loses weight before a dangerous lightning flash. But they were determined to go, and times were such that he could do little to stop them.

Both lay outside – others ready to follow when they had reached the ditch – a giant invisible hand holding them flat against the soil and withered autumn grass-blades. The hand lifted: they ran across the gap between wall and ditch on all fours like monkeys, one a few yards behind the other. Half way to the ditch they fell and were once more pressed into the soil for what to Evart seemed a long time. One of the escapers turned to see what lay on either side of him, and Evart glimpsed his face, a white mask with bloodless lips and eyes not too far away for him to detect in them the fear of an animal about to negotiate its last trap. What had they heard or seen that the others watching from the barn were not aware of? A gun fired from the hills, a low distant reverberation, a shell fired in sheer laziness it seemed, as a percussion to the whine and hum of insects. A hundred guns might save them, Evart thought, but one alone is a mockery.

Their bodies became taut for the last dash to the cover of the ditch. Armgardson in the barn stood ready to follow as soon as they dropped from view. They were within sight of the ruins along the road, and consequently slowed down their progress, hoping thus not to be noticed. One hesitated, stopped, and for some reason picked up a stone: the other went forward, and the one who had stopped began to move again, still holding the stone. There was an absolute silence in the barn that none of its occupants seemed to detect, being part of it.

The escapers reached the crest, and Armgardson was already squeezing his way out into the open. Evart watched those near the ditch and waited for them to roll into temporary safety. They did not move. Out there, he thought, they must have a hundred senses that we in the barn can't imagine existing. What do they feel? Why don't they move? And it occurred to him that the only difference between the violinist outside and himself within lay in the second hand moving over the various hidden faces of their watches, which went at different speeds, and stopped at unexpected times, in tune with each encased heart bent on deliverance.

The man with the stone pushed his arm forward until it touched the edge of the ditch, and those watching had their eyes on the stone he clutched rather than on his bodily movements. It was the stone that, when the firing began, was the only part of the escaping pair to find safety in the parched reeds below.

Late in the afternoon the doors were thrown open, and soldiers came in with cans of petrol, left them inside so that the flickering lamps could be filled. Lights grew white and strong, defeating shadows that bred repeat performances in every mind of the bloody and abortive attempt at escape earlier in the day. Another addition to comfort was some strong high-backed chairs and shining mahogany tables, a gift of plunder from the General that gave the orchestra an hour of debate on where to set them out among the bales. Such an incongruous mixture prevented anyone using the furniture for some time, having become accustomed to the more congenial straw, but eventually they moved towards it until, with a lamp set in the centre of a table, a few people surrounded it to play cards. It was a quiet game that generated only a low murmur of voices, a fact observed and pondered upon by Starnberg, who realized that here in their falsely settled community no kind of law existed. If anyone cared they could commit all kinds of crimes against each other, yet they desisted because a bigger crime had been collectively committed against them all. Here within their space of straw, furniture and flickering lights no one would lift a knife to kill because no other person among them had the power or inclination to give punishment. Did anyone hold a deep enough grudge to see this motion moving? Luckily no, for within the barn the word 'murder' did not exist, a crime only because a crime when there are ways of punishing it. These aphorisms turned into more logical truths: the reason why we are able to live here at peace is because we are too concerned with survival – or because we haven't yet been here long enough. When a group of people are able to live a normal life a killing not done for the sake of survival becomes a murder. Perhaps in the eyes of the Gorsheks the killing of the two violinists was unconsciously done for the sake of survival.

Evart ate slowly at supper, sitting as if in a small room by himself – until Starnberg broke the silence and joined him. 'We're being looked after like prize racehorses. Food excellent, guards courteous, even furniture given to us. The General's making sure he gets a good concert.'

'It was out of the question,' Evart said, frankly admitting what was on his mind, 'to stop them trying to escape. I somehow imagined that at the most they'd be recaptured and brought back. But it's impossible to predict what the General will do. It never occurred to any of us that he'd set guards on the roof to watch for an escape.' He reached for the plate of salt and sprinkled some into his bowl with the flattened handle of his spoon. Others had finished eating and were washing their bowls in drums of water near the door. The splashing of rain sounded from outside, and Evart noticed that when it turned into a tropical downpour the gangs of soldiers passing by did not run to avoid getting wet.

'I'm still hoping,' Starnberg said, pulling a roll of black bread into several pieces, 'that we'll get out of this place alive. I'm hoping most of all that the General's conscience won't let him do such a thing as slaughter us.'

'There's no such thing as conscience,' Evart said, pushing his empty bowl aside. 'There's fear, perhaps, that someone will do the same to you, and these people have lost that fear.' He felt for a cigarette and lit it. 'You've every reason to hope, though. I agree with your line of thought. Hope has nothing to do with reason, because the impossible can always happen. If and when it does it nearly always turns out to be something nobody had thought of.'

Starnberg went over to where he slept, tried to read some back issue of the orchestra's magazine, but was disturbed by heavy rain beating against the roof and walls. Together with the hollow-sounding guns it kept on most of the night. Everyone slept uneasily, talked in their sleep, cried out with each movement. Evart was conscious of being cold, for the heavy coat did not give much warmth against the dampness, and he felt himself towards dawn tugging at it and trying to cover himself completely, which could not be done. He dreamed a good deal, but could remember nothing.

In the morning the rain stopped, and showed a dull soaked landscape. A weak sun shone between low water-filled clouds that threw shadows on the distant hills, marking the shape and altitude of each ridge. Rain, to Starnberg, made everything seem more hopeless than it actually was. Or so he hoped. All hope is worthwhile, he told himself, whether anything comes of it or not. We don't hope because we want things to be all right – which would be nothing more than a trick – but because we have to hope.

Soldiers came in with more chairs, and cleared the barn in preparation for the General's concert that night. Starnberg stood up to help them, hoping as he did so that the concert would turn out to be their salvation.

9

The General hoped, as he came out on to the sunlit rooftop terrace of his house, that the concert would be a success. He stood with hands in pockets, looking away from the sound of gunfire, his eye catching the slow brown snake of a convoy coiling along a road towards a distant village. The sky had cleared except for grey cloud smudges on the fortified hills, and he wished the rain wouldn't return for some days so that extra reserves of ammunition could be carried to the front. Turning slightly, he saw that the main street of the village was now cleared of rubble, edged by shells of houses and the deposited slag-heaps of bricks and mortar. Farm buildings dotted beyond, having escaped the loop of destruction he had thrown around them, gave shelter to lightly wounded resting after the battle. In another part of the village gangs of impressed civilians were repairing houses for the winter, scurrying over them willingly enough, carrying straw baskets of cement and tiles, while in the centre square troops were standing in line to draw rations.

He was pleasantly moved by such signs of organization unfolding in every direction. The foothill masking positions were as perfectly dug, placed, supported and camouflaged as his knowledge and intuition could make them, for during the morning he had driven from one to another inspecting the most important. A few months would see the beginning of the 'big' offensive, and his anticipation of success made him impatient almost to the point of unhappiness. He had never previously known such a feeling in his pre-attack moods, and for the first time he began to label those that were less harmful: taciturnity, drunkenness, extensive planning that sometimes went on too long and contradicted itself, bringing on insomnia – but never impatience, never that cloven-hoofed quality that had sent so many commanders into exile.

Yet on thinking of the evening's entertainment – sounds of preparations for it came from the barn across the road – his mind was lightened to muted and more agreeable waiting that gave him access to unknown emotions. He had looked forward to symphonies as a young man – when they could still be played – but the one he would soon be hearing was divided from those by a gap measured more in events than time, and for him to explore this gap meant an immersion into milestones of slaughter and blood that had refused the minor poetic rhythms of music because they had no place in the art of war. Their absence had been felt, and he would experience their return with the depth and understanding given to him by middle age.

A sudden breeze turned him from the balustrade, so that he was again aware of activity in the barn – the harsh sound of instruments being tuned, movement of furniture, discussion over some no doubt insignificant crisis – and he closed his eyes as if to increase the comfort this noise gave him. The sound of war's preparation drifted away from his senses, and suddenly, on opening his eyes to the green plain and white houses beyond the village, he was faced with clear and cruel perspective by the fact that the orchestra which was to perform for him that night would have to be destroyed in two days' time.

He could not believe it, and only knew it to be true when the full history of High Command's order came back to him. He shielded his eyes, as if the sun were too strong for them, or as if to hide from his mind a ghastly vision of planned execution. These thoughts promised to destroy his enjoyment of the concert, and in a more reasonable mood he told himself that the orchestra would have been already dead had he followed High Command's order on first receiving the signal. I'm doing all I can, he justified himself from an abyss of weariness. A short, calm, isolated man, he stood by the parapet looking away from the house but taking in little now of the landscape detail: only an impressionistic confusion of colours worked their way into his cogitations. His mind went over the same facts like a too repetitive alliteration: the accidental capture of the orchestra, the decision submitted to High Command, the signal saying they were to be shot, and his capitulation to a slowly mounting desire to hear a symphony. Now he would hear one, the orchestra would be destroyed, and his life would go on as before.

Or would it? The wind increased. He put on his cap and paced slowly along the edge of the terrace, hands clasped behind, watching each boot of his foot as it went forward, lifting his head to see an enveloping camp that would not march until after rain and snow had covered the continent. Forgetting the orchestra he surrendered himself to the fascination of movement in the village and across country as far as his vantage point would allow him to see: at troop movements, supply columns and, over the hills, explosion-clouds lifting and joining to form a white scarf on dark grey slopes. Several bars of the symphony reached him, then gave way to the sound of gunfire. When the music came again he tried hard to fix each wavering note but the guns gained in power and finally drew him into their hard uneven rhythm. He paced up and down until he could listen to neither music nor gunfire and, on reaching a doorway, descended a dark tunnel-like staircase leading down into the house.

A group of Gorshek officers entered the brightly lit barn. They kept to themselves, smoking and talking in low voices by rows of chairs set out for them near the door. Seats for the orchestra, placed at the far end of the barn, were divided from those of the audience by a wide space of neutral ground on which no one cared to trespass. The floor had been swept and cleaned down to its earthen base, and bales of hay were stacked unobtrusively around the walls. Evart smiled sardonically at such good order, that helped to make an island of time in which the orchestra would play a symphony, where all thought of dying would be taken from them. He could hardly remember a concert, in fact, when they had been so light-hearted and lively before the performance began. One of the trumpeters shouted with a laugh: 'This is the first time I've ever played in a barn!'

'I hope it isn't the last time,' someone else called out ironically.

'I suppose they'll send in a few soldiers after the concert to help us put back the straw.'

A violinist told him: 'If you play your flute well enough it'll move back by itself.'

'We'll do it. It's an easy job. It'll give us something to do.'

'I'd rather charm the soldiers into doing it. I don't like work,' the other flautist said.

A sceptical voice exclaimed: 'No one can charm those barbarians.'

'Viccadi could, though,' Viccadi's friend retorted. Some did not speak, but stood among the chairs with instruments at their feet, or stayed at the back, quietly smoking in what little obscurity was left.

'There's a strange feeling in here,' Starnberg was saying, 'and most of them don't know what to make of it; neither the officers nor the orchestra. We haven't much heart to play this evening.' A bow scraped along strings and sent out a raw uneven sound, while a second violin, slowly mounting to a pitch of sweet clarity, was hidden by the raucous call of a trumpet.

'This'll be a good concert,' Armgardson remarked, and Starnberg winced inwardly at the sarcasm.

'I think they'll play well,' Evart ventured.

'Not that we want to,' Starnberg said, taking his violin from its case. 'We won't be able to do anything else but play well in a situation like this, if you see what I mean.'

'I don't want your noise,' someone said loudly to someone else.

Evart looked into the segregated orchestra. 'We all seem to have done nothing but sleep since we came here. We've done no work at all. I realize now that we should have rehearsed all the time, and offered to play this concert for the General, instead of waiting for him to ask.'

Some of the officers were now seated and talking more loudly. 'It comes to the same thing, more or less,' Starnberg said, lodging his violin between chin and shoulder then putting it down by his side again. 'But work never appealed less to me now. I only feel like lying down all the time and doing nothing.'

'Do we have time to smoke a cigarette before we start?' the drummer shouted.

'If you give me one,' said a thin, middle-sized man with a 'cello. 'I smoked my last yesterday.'

Starnberg saw the white flick of a cigarette thrown across chairs and over a man's dark hair, and then the 'cellist lift his hand to catch it. 'It's self-preservation that makes me want to lie down,' he said. 'I suppose one always feels safer like that.'

Evart rejoiced in the pause that followed, until conjecture of a damning sort rapidly filled it: self-preservation – an instinct forking two ways, leading to prolonged life or quick death, and the negative force of the latter still relevant because it perhaps preserves an even more important self of us in the long run, seen from the raw and exposed summit of those who chose life. Oh God, he thought, the worst thing is having a mind unable to embark on either one of the two courses. 'But if we play well,' he reminded Starnberg, 'it may lead to us not being killed.'

Starnberg sent a clear and undulating note out above the noise, then brought his violin down to tighten a key. 'This is hardly a symphony of hope we're going to play,' he said, forcing a smile.

'Best not to think about it,' Evart said. He went towards the chairs, calling out: 'No, I want you in this order. You three stay here and you others sit farther back.' They acted without question, something else he had not noticed before. 'It looks as though the General will be late,' he said, on coming back to Starnberg.

'It's his privilege.'

'Perhaps. But I'll start in five minutes whether he's here or not.'

'I imagine he's a punctual man,' Starnberg said. 'He'll be on time.'

'I'll never smoke these cigarettes again,' a voice from the second violins exclaimed. Someone struck the drums, and a dull ringing sound filled the barn. For a moment the officers stopped talking, then laughed. 'When I get home I'll smoke good cigarettes,' the same voice cried. 'I'll have a good time, to make up for this.'

'That's what frightens me,' Starnberg said to Evart. 'They still talk as if they're going back next week.'

Evart dropped a half smoked cigarette and pressed his heel into it. 'I hope they're right. I'm glad I've no control over such thoughts. Let them keep thinking that way. I'll be glad if something good comes of it.'

Starnberg began gladly to reinforce these statements, but Evart pushed by him and through the orchestra, walking to the wooden rostrum in front. He looked at them for a full minute, and on hearing the big wooden door open and close did not turn to see who had come in but continued to arrange the orchestra in their right places. The officers stood to attention, and the General told them to sit down.

When everything was still and there was no more noise

– even the gun-crews were given orders not to fire for the occasion – he turned and made a deep bow to the audience. Standing up straight, his baton down the seam of his trousers, he looked at the General and his officers for some time, seeing them perfectly still and waiting for the music to begin. He heard mixed noises of instruments at his back, the discordant realism of an orchestra tuning up at the last moment, noticing also that the only person in the audience unable to look at him was the General, whose eyes were turned to an empty corner of the barn. Is the fact that he's ashamed to kill us good or bad? Evart wondered, keeping himself perfectly erect, feeling the neatness of his hair brushed back over his head, the half discomfort of a newly unpacked suit, the sting where he had cut himself while shaving, and the energy in his body that made him glad they were going to play a symphony. The orchestra was silent and ready, so he turned abruptly and saw the first page of a full score below him, then tapped his baton twice as a signal that they were to begin.

A sound of strange music emerged from a pall of silence that covered the village. It was eerie and startling, like a brooding ghost coming in grave-clothes to haunt people who seemed to have forgotten its memory. It ascended, grew, until it filled the barn and tried, not quite in vain, to reach the outside air while still maintaining that pure clarity with which it left the orchestra. The General sat with legs crossed, looking into the folded hands in his lap as if to read the programme that his mind had cast there. The music, with greater ease now, oiled the rusty hinges of his memory, opened doors that led to his past, and he travelled along lanes of time, buffeted from one emotion to another, down a narrowing road that followed the calm beauty of music beckoning from a world he had too easily lost. Why did I? he asked. Because I chose to, he answered. And by making this question and answer he enjoyed the music even more as the symphony went on. Things that he

106

did not want to remember were brushed aside and banished into vague dreams, while other memories stood up clear and vivid, mocking the melodic line until he truly believed that he could reach out and live once more within this recreated fairy-tale past.

Starnberg lifted the page of his score, let it fall, and followed each note with the bow. Some notes signified a moment of hope as they were played, while others, revealing tiny areas of white where worn-out type had not been pressed home, became for him speckled moments of death displayed upon their oval heads, only forgotten by the transformation of each one into sound. Far from wanting to sleep, his one aim now was to keep on playing, to gamble on the high and low pitch of each note, and on the weight and progress of each bar, where everything was regulated and disposed of by the safe technical arrangement of time. 'Neither hope nor death exist while I'm playing,' he said to himself during a rest.

The General did not dare to move, seemed to be holding his breath until the end of a section, could not cough to clear the irritation in his throat, or shift his feet, or destroy someone nearby whose hand lifted for no reason.

With the end of the movement came a break filled by coughing from orchestra and audience, a stirring of papers, an adjustment of keys. No one spoke. The General pulled his hand down the side of his face, as if to waken himself, but gave up when the dazed dementia within would not be dislodged. Evart looked beyond the orchestra, towards the bars through which he could see nothing because he was too near the centre of light.

The storm of guilt began; a pursuit by sonorous beats, forerunners of thudding footsteps. Dark corridors were lit by no lamps, and the General's mind grew sombre as music came over him relentlessly, wandering against him one second, overwhelming him the next, until reality was drumming against the boundaries of incredibility. In such half sleep his divided brain was both for and against him, like a voracious sharp-toothed animal that had awakened in his body. With almost no pause came the dance, sensuous and moving, inopportune, almost humorous, yet latent with possibilities, becoming another and more subtle form of warning, as if to vanquish from every angle the heart he was discovering within himself. But he subdued it, crushed his thoughts from his mind after winning a fight that brought him greater heights of happiness than he had ever reached, allowing the innocent music to carry him along to the end of a movement.

Evart restrained his baton throughout the march. The score was filled with lanes of soldiers, each line a succession of blackened boots linked and unlinked in a uni-directional march, footsteps sloped in destruction, forming ranks of a private army filing into his brain; an army which, he was well aware, could defeat nothing. Each black boot was a beat of music slipping instantaneously from his imagination to the waving of his baton, a baton that signalled strict obedience to those boots whose continual march was taking him to the end of the symphony. Crashing and captivating, the General said with a smile, like the ideas that turned my head when I decided to join the Army.

Now I'd like to lie down in the quietest room of my own house, where there are no sounds of traffic, or guns, or people or music like this march; where there's no question of hope or despair, of living and dying, and of fear. Comfort and freedom is what we want, and cigarettes and more performances and women in big cities that we visit: all this to go on for a long time yet.

The officers were pleased with the march, and the loud pieces where drums dominated. When percussion was in control towards the end of the final movement they were stirred by the power and glory and promise of death (the reality of a quick finish without pain to the obstinate pleasure-loving body), and felt the delight of their General who sat in their midst. It brought a smile to their vacant faces, allowing them to move their hands under cover of its strength.

The lamp behind Starnberg drew down its flame and went out, and he read his score with difficulty in half darkness. The final music caught the General dwelling on one of the mass surprise attacks for which he had become famous; it dragged him like a gust of cannon fire from the pedestal on which he had set himself, and the barbarous loud rhythms flayed his mind and mocked him, showed the wake of an offensive: conventional signs of bloodied tree stumps and mounds of rubble, horizontal levels of burning ground, spot heights covered by the representative fractions of dismembered bodies, streams red with blood an hour after sunrise, lanes of fire and roads of smoke, scorched hachuring to mark the heightened elevation of his searching guns. Only blood and the ploughing of bombardment kept the land from becoming desert, was all the justification he could find. The music illuminated his vision, and its final symphonic beats synchronized his resignation to the slow steps of advancing fate.

He was standing up without knowing why. Unnecessary, he thought, clapping because his officers were already doing so, having realized what was needed of them before he lifted his hand. He stepped forward and faced Evart, began talking, running more words out from the last thoughts with him when the music ended. Clapping was in his ears: the General had liked it so much that they went on making their noise, and he never loved his officers more than at that moment, for he was able to curse and shout out the truth with no one else able to hear what he was saying.

He turned, pushed his way through the officers – who had already begun to leave – and walked out into the darkness towards the house lights. Fully awake at last he ascended the steps slowly and dejectedly, feeling heavy raindrops striking the sleeves of his tunic. A dog moved out of his path just as he had thought to kick it, and the guard saluted when he passed into the hallway. He turned the doorknob of the first office, the bewildered clerk standing rigidly to attention as he entered. The General walked to the table, turned the handle of the field telephone, and lifted the receiver, drumming on the tabletop with his fingers.

'Kondal?' he cried. 'See that the soldiers clean the barn.' He slammed the receiver down, held it for a few seconds then spun the handle again three times. 'You can commence your brigade's fire now.' He grunted at the acknowledgement, replaced the mouthpiece and walked out of the room, leaving the clerk to close the door after him.

He climbed slowly to his bedroom with a numbed blank mind, unable to think of anything very clearly (if someone had asked: 'Where were you five minutes ago?' he could not have answered them) until earth-tremors of exploding shells passed beneath his feet near the top of the stairs. Electric light bulbs swayed on the landing-roof, and on entering his room he saw blue flashes playing across the window before switching on the light. But the glare was too bright, burning his aching eyes, so he turned it off and undressed in the dark.

The crash and rumble of guns rattled the window panes, and colours of varying intensity spun across them. He found it impossible to sleep for some time. There was no end and beginning to his thoughts, and what fragments emerged – as if on a thin celluloid tape bound across his eyes – were either coloured or discoloured by gun-flashes against which he could not guard his vision. Nothing could keep the flames from reaching him: they entered the window and lit up every wall in the room, lurked in corners and roamed over the ceiling, burned his eyes when he opened them, bathed him in perspiration. There was no way of escaping the muffled synchronized sounds that pierced his half protected ears, though he turned from one side to another in an effort to do so.

Suddenly throwing back the clothes he reached for the telephone, filled with destructive rage that for the moment he could not unleash.

'Hello?' he shouted breathlessly. 'You can cease fire now.' He scowled in the darkness. 'Did you hear me? You can stop the bombardment now. Recommence a second-degree shelling at five in the morning.'

After hearing an apologetic voice repeat his orders he thrust the receiver back with such force that the table shook, then lay down again, pulling the clothes over him. He fell asleep in the silence.

10

Binocular-eyes roamed over a stretch of open terrain that had once been cultivated, beyond which rose foothills surfaced by patches of earth and scrub. With the naked eye it was difficult to see where ground dipped on the ascent, but with optical assistance many depressions were faintly discerned. Areas of lighter soil denoted ill-camouflaged pits, baited traps set for advancing infantry, and the black coin of a copse that had been burned out by incendiary artillery was now a fortified enemy position. Boulders and rocks, some with the remains of trees thrusting outwards singly or in clumps, were obviously dynamited, ready to be rolled down on any troops that might try to gain the summit. Above and behind these, not far from the rimline, lay a space of level ground defended by minefields, barbed wire and concealed outposts. Being the most precipitous part of the mountain range, with neither pass nor negotiable col, it was the least heavily defended, and it was here that the General's troops would ascend one night, clear the crest, and swarm down at dawn to the undefendable plain on the other side. Once over in strength they would veer south for several miles to the rear of the main pass and block the enemy's line of retreat. Anti-tank rifles would be carried by the second wave. Unable to withdraw, battered by armoured, gun and infantry assault from the front, the enemy would attempt to break out – and be annihilated in the process. Meanwhile, another Gorshek army sent in the tracks of the first would begin a flood-like advance to the east, leaving the pass beleaguered. When the pass fell, the advance would be swelled by an additional two hundred thousand troops. The success of this plan depended on a quick decisive breakthrough at this point north of the pass. Though a difficult part of the line to breach, it was equally difficult for the enemy to reinforce at short notice in face of a surprise attack, and once the pass had been captured the enemy would not be able to stop the Gorsheks until their old capital was reached. The General never lost sight of, and indeed made strong provision for, the possibility of advancing up to a thousand miles beyond, taking the Gorsheks once more into the heart of the eastern continent.

The forerunners of his attack, upon whom the success of his offensive depended, would be two battalions of fanatical men armed with long knives, creeping forward in the darkness. A single large shrapnel grenade would swing from each belt, all set to explode at the same time – when their carriers were fighting on the enemy positions. These explosions, distinctive in sound, would signal the normally armed battalions following behind to rush the crestline, while the enemy were still dismayed at the barbarous mass immolation of the advance guard. The Knife Battalions would not know what they carried, for the grenades were to be disguised as ration packs, with orders not to be opened until they were taking their first rest beyond the summit, by which time they would have done their work, in killing every man to which they were attached, as well as many of those against whom they would be fighting.

Instead of Knife Battalions it would have been easy to hold in readiness a number of those lives specially bred to volunteer death for the régime – in all the national armies there were many such units he could draw on – but for his deadset intricate purpose he wanted alert hardy groups of brave men who had no intention of dying. That was the subtle core of his trick, a facet of no great-seeming importance, yet one that the General intuitively felt would award success to his chain of stratagems.

The General raised his binoculars again, to the point

where his troops would blaze a mile-wide gap at the summit, looking at the place for a long time, like one animal facing another, as if to hypnotize the ground into giving an easy crossing when the time came. He tried to lift the binoculars higher, but the strap caught between his chest and the ledge of the car window. 'Kondal!' he called out, throwing the glasses down. He pulled a map from the driver's seat and made notes on the margin, marking small triangles and hachured escarpments between the wavy contours of the hillside. As soon as the path was clear, labour battalions would manhandle light guns up the mountain and reinforce the first troops fighting at the pass. The General realized how important it was that (a) the grenades of the Knife Battalions would not explode before they were with the enemy, and (b) that they would all go off at the same time. To hope for the latter was unreasonable, but at least they would produce a staggered ripple of noise to good purpose. Perhaps a rehearsal would help to make the plan more feasible, though he wondered whether it would be possible to do this without sacrificing another two valuable Knife Battalions as guinea-pigs in the experiment.

He looked at his watch and rolled up the thick-papered map, wondering: When will Kondal be back? He had left the car half an hour ago to look for signs of a battalion that was supposed to be guarding the wood. The General pushed the car door open, but it stopped at an angle of forty-five degrees, unable to swing back or go forward, to give room for him to step out, or close him in again. A dank life-giving smell of rain on leaves came from a nearby bush to emphasize the silence around him, a silence in which he was unable to believe, as if it were a continuation of the silence felt in last night's dream, surrounding him as he had climbed a mountain slope in half darkness, wading knee-deep for countless hours – it seemed – through bloody unbleeding limbs stained with dried grey mud, and never making progress. It had been an endless lonely scramble, that filled him with fear and rage when he woke up and realized the reason for his terror.

'Kondal!' he shouted, impatient to begin his inspection. 'Kondal!' He felt in his pocket for cigarettes and found he had brought none. Yesterday I wore no hat when attending a parade. I'm beginning to make mistakes, he thought sadly, leaning out of the car and shouting again towards the trees. 'Kondal! Kondal!' Shells began bursting a few hundred yards south-east, fired from guns on the southern edge of the wood. He leaped out of the car and walked to the back where the radio was installed. A thorn bush caught his ankle and he kicked it blindly away, turning the three-pointed switch to 'Transmission' and unfastening the microphone.

'Sixteen battery?' he called. 'GOR 16?'

He was answered, and demanded to speak to the battery commander. 'Don't fire any more until midday, then fire your guns at random within effective range. I'm at 069196 on a tour of inspection and don't want return fire coming down on the wood.'

The shelling ceased. Birds that had been disturbed by the noise returned to their high precarious nests of wartime. A pine cone dropped from a tree on to hard ground, and he heard the dulled cracking of twigs nearby. Kondal appeared from between the trees.

'Didn't you hear me call you?' the General demanded.

'The guns were firing, your excellency,' Kondal explained, his salute an awkward movement because of the arms he carried. 'And I was too far away to hear you.'

'You're a dull-witted idiot then, and shouldn't have stayed away for so long, and a liar as well, because I shouted for you long before the guns began. You must have heard me.'

Both stood near the back of the car, and Kondal's face was pained and apologetic, as one who deserved the abuse he was receiving. 'I went some distance into the wood,' he said, 'to see if I could find any sign of the soldiers. I searched for a long time, because the undergrowth is thick like it is in the southern forests, and suddenly I found them not far from where we are now. They didn't see me because I went towards them quietly.' Tugging firmly at the strap of his shouldered automatic rifle he pointed out the direction. But the General, having listened to his speech, ignored him now and walked to the car for his maps. 'Show me the way,' he said, slamming both doors shut.

The path was ankle deep in rotting leaves and, though wading through them, the General did not notice the noise they were making, or the direction in which they were walking, for the edge of the wood was soon left behind. Time and distance passed in a half dream for him, so that for all he knew miles were moving beneath his feet and days flying away from his life. Kondal took several turnings in the path – the presence of which only he seemed to feel beneath the mass of leaves – to avoid hillocks. The General looked up from time to time, seeing Kondal always a few yards in front, a protective helmet set roundly on his regulation-like head, and a rifle resting comfortably against his back.

Kondal stopped, and listened.

'How far now?' the General asked in a low voice.

'We're here, your excellency. We've only to climb a bank in front and their positions are behind it.'

'Then go forward quietly,' the General said, recognizing the sloping scrub-covered rampart. 'No one has heard us yet, and I want to see how effective their guard system is.'

Kondal objected. 'If we go too quietly we may be shot. They'll think we're an enemy patrol. Whereas if we call out and walk in openly they'll hear us coming and won't be tempted to shoot.'

The General unclipped his revolver and pointed it at

Kondal's back. 'Go forward,' he hissed. 'Do what I tell you.'

Feeling the hard muzzle pressed against him, Kondal crept between the bushes, making no sound. The General followed, pushing some leaves away from his face, thinking: If we get shot to death it'll solve a problem, for then someone else will have to kill them. Why do I have to carry out such a terrible job? How did the situation arise? I don't know. I forget. Why did it have to hang itself around my neck? A question came to him with each slow footstep: How can I find some way of keeping them alive? Is it possible without High Command finding out? The ground rose beneath his feet. They were ascending the bank, zigzagging to its crest. No, he told himself, it isn't possible. I've already committed a grave breach of discipline by keeping them alive for so long, when the signal said in plain and simple words that they were to be killed immediately.

Standing on the flattened earth of the rampart, Kondal turned to make sure he was still there. Soldiers were heard muttering incoherently, as if just waking from sleep, some picking up their guns, others drawing knives, all in a desperate silence as if thinking they were about to be attacked yet not having the will to do much about it.

'Where are the guards?' Kondal roared, stepping down from the bank and pointing his rifle at them. They replaced their arms, moved back as he walked among them, and, seeing the General, stood to attention like petrified men.

'Where's your officer?' the General demanded of the nearest soldier, who was about to answer when footsteps were heard coming from the wood, and the General saw an officer leading a patrol into the redoubt. Each man's face was haggard, their clothes damp and soil-stained, and they came forward wearily, tired under the weight of equipment. From the back of the last man waved the thin aerial of a radio set. One by one they sat down, not realizing that the General was nearby.

These are the men who should be killed, not the orchestra. I have to murder ninety musicians, and this rabble must be considered sacred. 'Why didn't you post sufficient sentries?' he asked, when the officer came towards him and saluted.

'But they are posted, your excellency,' he answered in a surprised tone.

'Where? I haven't seen them,' the General said sarcastically.

'I sent them to the stream on the southern edge and to the north-west,' he was told. The General pulled a leaf from a nearby bush, pressed its brittleness to powder with his fingers, felt the heat of rage in his eyes, and blood racing through limbs that must spend their force on something. 'We've had patrols out to the east as well,' the officer went on, standing in silence to prepare for the burst of anger that could be seen in the face before him.

'And are your patrols out now?' the General shouted.

'I've just led one in.'

He roared, stepping nearer so that the officer felt breath against his face: 'We've just come from the road and didn't meet either a patrol or sentry of any kind. Neither did we hear any sound of a patrol in action. I want you to test the defences on the hillside and send me your reports. I want all the information you can get on the terrain in this area. Well?' he raved, each word echoing through the trees. 'Send out another patrol. Keep your men active. Get some life back into them.'

The officer turned to obey the order, but his men were unable to stand. The General went to the nearest group and kicked out with his heavy boots, crying: 'Get up. Don't you know when to do what you're told? Come on, start moving.' Silently, hypnotized by his rage, they shouldered their rifles and prepared to move off.

Kondal stared hard from motionless yet all-seeing eyes. 'Don't you know we're at war?' he asked. 'Well, we are. You're not in a rest camp.' He laughed at the wildness of his remark. 'Come on: get up.' The General, seeing darkening embers at the base of a tree, turned again on the officer: 'Why did you make a fire? Do you want to light a beacon for the enemy's guns? I don't want too much attention drawn to this wood.' The officer's face remained grave. 'With a dozen men I could have slaughtered your whole battalion in a few minutes. During the night I could have done it with less, for I suppose you were sleeping. Don't you realize that you're ordered to stand-to all the time?'

'During the night, your excellency,' the officer answered, 'two-thirds of my men were patrolling the hills. Two of the patrols haven't come back yet.' He stood a foot taller than the General, yet looked down on him in fear.

'No,' the General exclaimed, 'of course they haven't come back. And they won't either, because they're such inefficient soldiers that they don't know how to take care of themselves.' He looked wildly around the clearing, as if searching for more accusations to throw against him. 'And your reports? What about the information your patrols gained during the night? Or were they too observant for their own safety to bring me any?'

'I've already sent the morning's intelligence to head-quarters, excellency, by special messenger,' the officer said calmly.

'You should have sent it by radio.' It's so obvious that they should have, the General told himself; but I might just as well be speaking to them from an unbridgeable world of my own. They're still digesting the hardship of the last battle and will need at least a month before they are recovered from it.

The officer's reply was mildly contradictory, though made in a reasonable voice. 'I was afraid of it being intercepted by the enemy, your excellency.'

Kondal unslung his gun. The falling forward of its safety-catch dominated the pause. The General's continuing rage came as a relief: 'Do you think I give orders for nothing? I wanted you to send it by radio, hoping the enemy would pick it up. I want them to see we have an equal interest in every part of the front.'

'I thought it was too important to send by radio,' the officer said quickly, caught between a desire to placate the General and a wish to avoid an argument that would arouse Kondal to action. 'Some of my soldiers went to the crest last night without being seen, and observed enormous reinforcements of the enemy moving up from the distance. The whole area was a sea of lights.'

He's lying. They never show lights. Yet the General noted his remarks. Perhaps so. Maybe a winter holding attack would be in order if he's correct. With these men?

'But my instructions?' he cried out. 'Why were they disobeyed?'

The question was unanswerable. The General saw for the first time the wretched men against whom he was raving, whose faces were characterless but for the endurance and bravery deepened into them. From under each helmet eyes looked through the pure air of fatigue. Some shivered in the cold damp atmosphere, leaned against the nearest tree, afraid to rest on it completely because they knew that he was looking at them. One man lay huddled by the bole of a tree, his body choking and rattling, his eyes glowing with fever as if the few hours of life left to him had collected there to make a last stand. Everyone was fixed into a tableau, waiting for the General to speak or move.

'What's your battalion strength?' he asked the officer.

'A hundred and ninety-three, your excellency.'

He detected a strange glint in the eyes of the men around him. At the end of long marches he had seen it, during the great retreats that he had endured in his younger days, when the land had been swept clean of every root and nothing but human flesh stood between a spark of life and starvation. 'Where do you bury your dead?' he asked.

It was something he had never done himself, but knew the smell of such and the look it left in men's eyes, the poisonous paralysing stare and gait it gave them, marking the death of their intelligence, the death of reason for any higher purpose than that of tracking, killing, reloading automatic weapons and killing again. And it often happened that once they had developed a taste for it normal food became repugnant.

'What do you do with your wounded?' he demanded.

The officer looked blankly before him as if he were asleep. The others stared uncomprehendingly, and the General knew that if he stood there for a century he would get no answer. 'Are your food supplies adequate?'

'Yes, your excellency.'

'Even so, I'll double your rations.'

He tapped Kondal on the back and they walked towards the edge of the clearing, entered the bushes and descended into the trees. Dead twigs cracked under their feet, and through the roof of foliage a grey-white sky made a higher roof. It seemed to him that Kondal, though happy, did not even know he was happy, but simply stalked in front with his neck bent forward as if leading a patrol towards a concealed outpost, possessed by the thrill of knowing that death could reach out at any moment. Such ease of mind, such nonentity of spirit, seemed the height of insubordination to the General, though he had to admit that Kondal was in no way a fool. He just hasn't reached the stage of knowing that decisions involve much more than instinct, he said to himself; and he never will, though he's intelligent for all that, and lucky in having nothing to oppress him. Aren't I happy, too? My feet are treading down dead leaves; I can hear a patrol setting out from the clearing we've just left; my limbs take pleasure in moving through

121

this quiet wood, and I'm happy knowing that there's a range of hills nearby with an army on them, and that in the spring I'll set my plans going in order to destroy that army, even to wipe out what reinforcements they might hold in readiness for me. But my brain isn't happy because the orchestra are lodged there, tearing and ripping it with lion's claws.

He suddenly stopped, though Kondal continued walking, not noticing the absence of his footsteps. What am I to do? he asked himself. How can I keep them alive? His eyes mimeographed the signal, received from High Command before leaving his office: REQUEST CONFIRMATION OF EXECUTION OF NONCOMBATANTS RE YOUR ENQUIRY URGENT.

A hammerblow to smash the mind, a reminder of the mind's division, that feels like the cut of a surgeon's scalpel on unkilled, unethered flesh. The split between past and future, and I have to make up my mind quickly. It's as though I've been made my own god. There's nothing I can do. I might already have been marked down for exile, though I can disguise my delay if they're shot now. Rifle-fire is coming from the hills but these woods are silent. I can't hear the noise of the patrol any more, and Kondal is out of sight, and the music of my guns won't support this argument, though I suppose I'm magnifying my problem until it seems I'm on the pinhead of the world's destiny, or something foolish like that. Am I? Ridiculous. Of course not. I'm a soldier, not a martyr. I want to die for myself, in excitement, preferably in a battle, smashed in one second by bomb or shell, not for a cause in desolation, dying in the fungus of some tree bottom like the soldier in the clearing. I gave them two days to live after the concert, didn't I? Wasn't that enough? (Isn't two days the same as two hundred years?) I should have had them killed this morning. If only they weren't still alive!

He moved again, walking forward cautiously.

'Kondal!' he shouted, making his way to where he

122

thought Kondal should be. Why has it suddenly come upon me like this? I'm a soldier. Isn't it easy to give an order, even if it's an impossible order? One has only to speak a few words and it's all over, finished. You pick up a telephone and say . . . and say . . . No, you don't even think about what you're going to say. 'Shoot them,' you say. And that would be that.

'Kondal!'

There was a dearth of rifle shots, a drought of ghostly echoes in the wood, a scarcity of footsteps sounding as soft as shadows, a destitution of gunfire on both sides of the front; but the General felt like a man besieged, set on by every noise and movement. All my officers know that I have this problem: I bully them and they keep out of my way: I kick my soldiers and feel their dim hate burning my boots. No one can or will help me, and in any case they wouldn't dare to try! The trees are Kondal's friends because they make him feel safe and well hidden from stray bullets, but they stop me from seeing my way clearly across a plain of thorns. He's lucky to have such a heavy lid on his intelligence. These trees burn me with their incriminating branches. They're my enemies. I'd send five hundred of my soldiers up those hills to a useless death, if I could save the orchestra.

Kondal had waited for him among the trees.

'Go on,' the General ordered. 'Walk on.'

He pushed a branch out of the way, let it spring back on to the empty path. There's no problem for me. I can't let them live, simply because I've received an order for their execution. These personal feelings don't count, they're private to my mind and must stay there, dead. If I disobey the order I'll be exiled and sentenced to live as a convict, and someone else will be given the job of killing them. There's nothing I can do. They'll be killed whatever happens.

They reached the edge of the wood. A patrol, like an

irregular line of brown dots stippled among boulders and gorse, was crossing open ground high up the hillside. They passed a clump of trees, and the General watched them through binoculars, foreseeing from where he was the ambush that sprang upon them. He heard the dulled noise, an extra dimension suddenly appended to the stippled design, throw out sharper echoes around neighbouring ravines and clefts – and saw the soldiers falling to earth. Two survivors made their way down between limestone bluffs, coming to tell of another defence post not noticed before. He took a bearing on it with his prismatic compass. I'll send in some reserves: these men are worn out. A labour brigade can dig tunnels under the wood to hold the Knife Battalions. But the officer had spoken of reinforcements – a sea of lights – should he alter his plans then? It could be a trick, that they're intended for another part of the front. Great patience would be needed to find out their true intentions.

Throwing the map into the back of the car, he said: 'Drive me to the village. I want some lunch.'

The car followed rut-tracks along a lane, turning later on to a recently repaired road, where Kondal drove along its centre like a happy man who had not held a steering wheel for many years. He swerved from one side to the other until, hearing the General's shout above the engine noise, he settled down to a more moderate speed. The fields on either side looked as though they had been beaten into submission before being robbed of their harvest; they were lifeless and without colour under the greying sky, and trees were fixed like old thin hands into the landscape. Pressed back against his seat, legs stretched out as far as the build of the car would allow, the General speculated desperately on what he would like to do regarding the orchestra, and what he must do, and the numberless possibilities always spiralled back to the same point of departure: that he must have them shot. The death of his conscience would pass unnoticed in the intense paper-work necessary for preparing the spring offensive, and reforming his plans should the officer's assessment of enemy reinforcements against this part of the line turn out to have been accurate.

At the next turn of the road the car became entangled among a northbound convoy. For a while Kondal ran the car at great speed along a grass verge to avoid the first stream of lorries, then followed an erratic style of weaving that brought him to a halt.

'Why have we stopped?' the General asked.

Kondal pointed out of the window, at a road blocked with lorries.

'I'd better see what's the matter, or we'll be here all day.' The General got out and walked to the nearest lorry, enquiring for the traffic officer. 'In the one behind,' he was told, in such a casual way that Kondal, who followed, quickly assumed an appropriate and serious expression for the scene that was to come. The General stopped at the lorry, shouting, 'Is the traffic officer in there?'

An officer descended from the high cab and stood before him. 'So you're the fool responsible for these lorries blocking the road? Why don't you make up your mind which side they're to travel on?'

'The lorries are going at regulation speed, sir,' he replied, unable to understand the rank of the General. Kondal told him to whom he was speaking.

'Is it part of the regulations,' the General vociferated, 'to travel in two lanes down the road so that no other vehicle can pass?'

The officer did not reply. Kondal looked up and down the line of lorries. Drivers were leaning out of their cabs and staring at the disturbance. He felt a drop of rain fall coldly upon his cheek, thought that he might be hungry, and heard the General shouting: 'Is it? Why don't you speak? Are you dumb, you fool? Why don't you answer me?'

11

Sunlight came through two cracks in the barn wall, looking to Evart like the deceptively fragile antennae of some giant insect about to break down the walls and enter. His bones ached from the cold, as though knives were lodged between them, but when he turned to go back to sleep, and it seemed as if the knives moved, he said to himself: At least I'm still alive. Two lamps had been left burning, the weaker gleam of one spreading an indistinct shadow over Starnberg's face, showing his down-curved lips and closed eyes.

Evart gave up trying to sleep, for his body was too stiff and his eyes had already reintroduced themselves to daylight, and too much noise came from the nearby road. He eased himself up from the floor and folded his damp coat across two suitcases, then turned out the lamp.

Starnberg's eyes stared at the beamed and cobwebbed ceiling. 'I forgot to put it out before going to sleep.'

'I'm sorry I woke you.'

'You didn't. I've been awake since five o'clock.' He sat up, breaking each sentence with a yawn. 'But I kept my eyes closed hoping it would hold some of the warmth in!' A splashing of water sounded as someone washed himself at the buckets, and a man lying near to Starnberg brooded to his friend on nightly flea attacks that filled his sleep with awful dreams, though adding with determination that he would get rid of them today.

'Why do that?' his friend laughed. 'They'll run away from all of us after tomorrow morning.'

'You're a bloody fool to say such a thing. You know very well it's been settled that we'll be all right.' He picked up a

126

towel and walked to the buckets by the door, before his friend could shout out more verses of what was commonly regarded as distorted truth.

'No one thinks of escaping now,' Starnberg speculated. 'I suppose it's too much of a risk.'

Evart waited a long time between draws of his cigarette, as if it were filled with some drug and he was testing each rising stage of its effect. 'Why don't *you* try to escape?' he said at last.

Starnberg answered simply: 'Because I don't want to get shot. I'd rather wait and see if I can get out of it without violence. But what about you? You're probably the only one of us cool enough to make a success of it.'

'I'll wait with the rest. In any case, I can't see anything worth escaping for.'

'I don't understand.'

'Well, where would I go?'

'Back over the hills, of course,' Starnberg smiled, as though he were answering questions in some kind of game.

'No I wouldn't because there's nothing left for me over there. Which is why I won't try to get away.'

'It's senseless to think that.'

Evart sat down. 'It'd be senseless if I thought there was anything left,' he said. 'We are forced into this situation by people who tell us they're fighting for our freedom. Do you think I'm such a fool as to want to go back to that freedom when the same may happen again? Being captured has made me realize that there's very little difference between that civilization, and this "method of life" that our side are so busy fighting.'

'I don't agree. At least the life we've left isn't strange to us, and we can make a tolerable existence in it. I want life at any price, and if I went back over those hills I'd have it at a fairly good price.'

Neither spoke for a few minutes. Someone swore loudly because he had lost a razorblade, which meant searching among deep straw to find it. Several men were arguing by the door as to who would be the first to use a bucket of water, and they began shouting and threatening to hit each other. In a sudden scuffle the bucket was tipped over and they stared at the spreading water in silence, like children who had broken a precious toy. They shouted recriminations at each other, but the noise soon subsided.

'What would you do, then?' Starnberg recommenced, 'if we were suddenly sent back under truce?'

'Make the best of it, like everyone else.'

The doors swung open and two guards pushed in a trolley loaded with bins of steaming oatmeal. Men walked from all parts of the barn to meet it and to enjoy cool gusts of fresh air that came in at the same time. They saw lorries and cars drawn up outside the General's house, and officers loitering in groups on the wide space in front. Edging closer to the doorway they laughed at a soldier chasing ducks back towards a pond from which they had strayed. Two peasant women shuffled up to the house carrying eggs and vegetables, watched by a soldier who was on the roof repairing telephone cables, his head tilted against patterns of blue sky and cloud.

Breakfast was unloaded, the trolley taken away. The guards loitered for some minutes before closing the doors. A black kitten that had come in with them was left behind, and mewed at the spot where they were eating, scratching the table leg with its front paws until a bowl of food was set down for it. The men, as they ate, were either morosely silent, or arguing bitterly. A noisy group surrounded Armgardson.

'Use your imagination,' he was shouting hoarsely. 'You've been captured by atrocity-mongers. You're not in a café having your boots cleaned.'

'Sit down,' a 'cellist cried. 'You're making everyone nervous. You talk as though you're a gospel of truth.'

Armgardson leaned across the table, fair lank hair slopping over the side of his face. 'Are we going to sit here and wait to be killed like so many sheep then?' he bawled into the face of his interrupter.

'Be quiet and leave us alone.'

'Are we then? Are we?' he roared again. Several sarcastic remarks were made that he did not or chose not to hear.

'You don't know what you're talking about,' the man beside him said. 'Nobody's going to be killed: we did too well at the concert. They'll keep us prisoner as long as we play now and again. They're only barbarians to their own people.'

Cries of assent came to this. 'Of course! Of course!'

'If they keep to the agreed time set after the concert, none of us will be living tomorrow,' a voice reminded them.

Armgardson looked for the person who had thus come to his aid, but could not find him in the encircling crush, though he smiled happily at hearing a point of view that tallied with his own.

'We can only wait and see what happens,' was a voiced sentiment with which most of the others agreed. Armgardson scowled, threw a spoon on to the table with such force that it made a series of jumps away from him and fell on to the floor. He looked at the faces round about – then pushed his way forcibly through them, crying: 'You talk and act as if you've nothing to live for.'

'We've got as much to stay alive for as you have,' someone shouted into his face. He walked to the back of the barn and stood alone by the window, looking through the bars. Evart had heard their argument, and had seen the long legs of Armgardson stride angrily by when it was finished. The barred window was like a shrine before which nearly everyone had stood since they were imprisoned, and the scene it framed was an altar that had replaced any gods they might have believed in before they came to the barn. Evart had often seen them praying silently into it, unable to give offerings from their empty hands. Pushing the bowl aside he walked over to Armgardson and stood by him until he was noticed.

'Why aren't they all weeping?' Armgardson asked, his rough suffering face pressed to the wall.

'Because they don't think they're going to be killed,' Evart replied, putting a hand on his shoulder.

'Or is it because their own blind natures preserve them from weeping?' Armgardson suggested. 'It won't let them know the truth.'

'We should be glad then. I think they all know what's going on, so let them eat their food and play cards, read books and sleep. It's no use worrying anyone.'

Armgardson drew back and faced the window, still not looking at him. 'I wasn't disturbing them. One can't help getting into an argument. I forgot how it started in fact.'

'We don't know what's going to happen yet,' Evart said, offering him a cigarette, 'so it's best to keep quiet.' Having waited for him to take a light he walked to the other end of the barn. The doors were open again and guards were bringing in water. The sun, now in full strength above the opposite housetops, came in like a flood, giving hope, encouragement and warmth. Men in shirt-sleeves walked to and from buckets carrying towels and razors, joking, talking, the stricken pallor gone from their faces. These were the times of their greatest hope, when they did not believe that anything so terrible as death could happen, when they unconsciously imagined that they were here on earth for eternity, or that when death did come they would be so old that it would either be a relief to go, or would pass unnoticed. In the meantime they stood in the warm cushioning sun, pleasurably aware of the receding chill on their arms and faces after the enlivening bite of fresh water.

They cleaned their bowls and scoured the tables. Two men carried a drum of fuel around the barn refilling lamps; others brushed a clean gangway through the straw. 'They're a long way from losing hope,' Starnberg said to Evart. 'They've started a lottery. Someone made a book of numbers and each one costs a cigarette. The man who has his number drawn from Bender's 'cello case wins them all.'

'A good idea,' Evart said. 'I hope he'll enjoy his smoking.' It was worth something certainly; the end of it was an indication of breath, an easy interpretation of a hieroglyphic formed by the smoke that said: I live, I live. 'What's the matter? Why are you laughing?'

Starnberg unscrewed the top from his lamp and began to rub it with a rag, breathing against the glass in the same meticulous fashion as when he cleaned his spectacles. 'It's the first time I've heard you use the words: "I hope"; I'm encouraged quite a lot when it comes from you, even if it is the slightest bit ironic.'

'I'd like to persuade myself that it meant something,' Evart said, 'but I absolutely can't.'

'You use the word unconsciously,' Starnberg smiled, 'which means that you unconsciously hope, and there's far more truth in that than if you'd slowly persuaded yourself by reason.'

It was a far-fetched hypothesis, this clinging on to a single word, one of many that were bound to come out in unguarded moments. Could there be any oracular truth in it though? Evart asked himself. A variable chastened noise of gunfire came from the front, but the orchestra had lived within range of its phonetic mutterings for so long that it was only noticed now when deliberately listened for. 'Yes, perhaps I am beginning to hope, but I don't know why, for there's certainly no reason to.'

'Reason!' Starnberg exclaimed. 'What's that got to do with it?'

'It's like a game of cards,' Evart said. 'There's a chance, and that's all.'

'Of course,' Starnberg admitted on further reflection, 'I

think most of the men here have some reason for wanting to stay alive, for I've seen many of them writing letters to their families and friends which they'll post, they say, as soon as they're able to. You can't have greater faith than that in such a situation, especially from this wild godforsaken stretch of the world.'

'I wonder what they're writing?'

'Probably that they'll be coming back soon, and that they aren't being treated badly.'

'I can't share such optimism,' Evart said.

'But you can share their hope,' Starnberg told him. 'And it's hope that matters now, not sanity.'

'Have you written *your* letters yet?'

Starnberg looked dully at the floor, and seemed not to have heard. Evart turned away, and saw Armgardson pick up the black kitten to stroke it. When it leapt out of his arms and made slowly for the rear wall Armgardson went down on his haunches to call it back; but with fine precision the cat measured the distance to the bars, and sprang upwards on to the ledge, from where it turned and looked at everyone, daring them to pursue it. Armgardson walked a few paces forward and, when he sensed that the kitten was going to leap outside, picked up a piece of wood, which he threw with all the force of his muscles at the window. The cat leapt nimbly on to the grass, and the wood made a ringing noise when it bounced against iron. Voices cried out that he should leave it alone.

Evart said, almost to himself: 'I think he's insane. Armgardson threw a piece of wood at the cat.'

'Oh. I didn't see it. I was thinking about your question. You're right. I haven't written any letters, and I was wondering why. But I don't know why, though I'm sure I've as much hope of getting out of this as anybody else. I hadn't even thought of writing a letter. It simply didn't occur to me. The only writing I've done has been some notes on our imprisonment in this place, but nothing else.'

'Are you going to write any?'

'I don't think so. Not at the moment.'

'Why not?'

'Perhaps because I have more hope than optimism. It may be that I hope for life at the moment and nothing else, then when I have a promise of life again I can afford to be optimistic.'

Evart rolled up his shirt sleeves, and took a towel from his case. Then, as if forgetting his intention to shave, he leaned against the bale of hay thinking that there was no reason for hope, that the executions, as far as anyone knew, were set for the following morning, though everyone assumed – having been given no right to assume – that they would not take place. Was this collective assumption the intangible evidence of what was going to happen? Why was it that, having been clearly sentenced to die, the majority of them thought no more about it, and went on as if perfectly confident that they would live through the experience as prisoners? But it was his fancy, he told himself. Perhaps it's I who's insane, conjuring up this mystical feeling and turning it into a prophecy for good when no such feeling exists. For really, there's no more reason to hope now than when I first came back from the interrogation and told them what the General had said. Yet he saw clearly that hope was among them, that they seemed happy in living with it. He realized too that there was hope in himself, that he had caught it from the others perhaps, and he marvelled at the unobtrusive mechanics of contagion. The noise around him was not noise that came from condemned men: it was the noise of prisoners with the hope of liberation, a general expectancy of impending and favourable events. Hope seemed to be coming in on the low hum of the wind, to exist in the sounds of working from the village and from the house opposite, and even out of the echoing vociferations from the hills. It was a living force in the air, until you heard it in the silence of darkness

133

and saw it in the soft light of the lamps that were lit in the evening, and in the shadows that they cast upon the walls.

Starnberg took out the exercise book in which he inscribed his notes. This afternoon – perhaps because it was afternoon – he had no desire to open it, yet before he could justify any more delay he had written: 'There is very little spirit left among us. Only Two-metres walks his cage like an animal that senses freedom to be near. But what kind of freedom will it be?'

Then he stopped. Two days had passed since the concert. It had not been very pleasant waking up that morning. Most of them had accepted the fact that they were not going to die, but the few who thought it might be possible kept quiet and said nothing. As soon as Starnberg's closed eyelids sensed that it was getting light he had opened them so as to live through the whole dawn just in case, and he felt those others, who were also not sure, opening their eyes as well. He had thought that if he were going to die he would like it to get light slowly, but also that he wanted the light to make up its mind one way or another so that he could be certain that life was to go on. It had been an enigma that taxed his senses a hundredfold, an enigma that he did not like, because for several uneasy minutes it took complete control of him so that he felt like some ghostly puppet possessing just enough sense to know that it was about to be moved – without knowing which way. But light came into the barn, the hand of his watch travelled slowly, and his only thought when dawn had passed was one of disappointment because there was no sun.

After breakfast the indomitable card school gathered at the largest table, a circle of poised hands and bent heads playing with cigarettes as stakes. The doors stayed open the whole morning, and Starnberg for some reason wished they had been kept closed, for they left no barrier between them and the merciless rain that elbowed its way down to earth, creating pools and filling gutters, and generating a smell of dampness that suggested decomposition in the numberless half buried bodies scattered about the plain.

In the cigarette lottery each duplicate ticket became an exciting event as it was made into a ball and rolled like a head into Bender's 'cello case. One head was picked out to keep on living, drawn by Starnberg as a non-smoker. It belonged to Evart and brought in its train a hundred cigarettes. They laughed at his luck as he handed them around, and they spoke of a trick that Starnberg had no doubt played, of engineering a prize for Evart so that Starnberg could take his place as leader of the orchestra after he had smoked himself to death.

The black cat, Evart said, had brought him the prize, not Starnberg's trickery, for the cat had stayed with them much of the morning. Few of the orchestra knew how it happened: Evart saw Armgardson standing with the cat in his hands by the barred window, and to Evart the continuous and regular motion of Armgardson's fingers lifelessly moving along its smooth fur, together with his prolonged stare towards an empty part of the barn, seemed somewhat menacing. Yet so could many minor actions of men in this situation – and he thought little of it. Until suddenly a quick piercing scream from the cat cut through the barn, and, almost simultaneously, one decisive blow that killed it. Armgardson looked at the dead animal he was holding.

They were appalled at what he had done, for the kitten had become a favourite with them, eating the scraps left at each meal. Why had he killed it? Evart wondered. It hadn't been unsociable, and was the one friend they had made since being captured. Those who were superstitious said that Armgardson had killed whatever luck they might have had. Two men threatened to hit him, but when he stood up against them with raised fists they became afraid and left him alone. He threw the kitten as far as he could out of the window, but went back to look at it from time to time, to make sure it had not miraculously come to life and walked away. They said he was insane.

Subdued, tired and weary with inactivity no one prophesied any more what was going to happen, and half written letters stayed forgotten in pads and pockets. The books they brought with them, going quickly from hand to hand, began to fall apart, and Starnberg wondered what they would do when there were no more books to read, or cigarettes to smoke, or cards to play. Perhaps they'll simply sleep, he thought; or most likely they'll find something else to do. Like everyone he detested the waiting and uncertainty. If only they'd tell us one way or the other, he said to himself, whether we're going to be killed, or just remain here as prisoners – or be released from the orbit of this demoralizing captivity.

The guns began at midday. As soon as they stopped to the north they commenced in the centre, and a few minutes after they ceased firing in the centre they began in fury to the south, each bombardment lasting eleven minutes exactly, like a dull whip combing the hills; like the grumbling of the General's anger, as if he didn't know what to do with the orchestra. Another torture had been devised: previously, all guns had been placed in positions between the village and the front line, but now several monstrous pieces began firing from behind, so that shells and rockets furrowed the air overhead at irregular intervals. Starnberg walked to the window to breathe some fresh air, for the atmosphere within was dull and heavy. The cat's body lay on the grass, drops of water flattening its fur, a sight that disturbed him, for no matter how much he tried to avoid it, his eyes always went back to it. He wished Armgardson had not gone insane.

After midday Kondal came in and demanded a list of the players' names in the orchestra. 'For my records,' he said. Evart told him brusquely that no list was available, but Kondal maintained firmly that he wanted one, immediately, and his eyes moved dangerously when Evart said that he wouldn't even give one to the General. The others pressed close to Kondal, not realizing, after their experience by the train, that he might be a man who continually suffered from claustrophobia due to his having developed a too easy recourse to firearms in such situations. He took out a revolver and thrust it forward, shouting that they move back and stop clamouring. He again demanded a list of names, and Evart refused. Kondal pointed the revolver directly at his face. 'Give it to me,' he said with an amiable grin that made Starnberg shudder, 'or I'll kill you.'

When Evart faced him without speaking Kondal did not know what to do, being aware that the General, for some reason he did not understand, regarded these prisoners as sacred and not to be handled violently. But there was a narrow limit to Kondal's patience and understanding. He approached Starnberg: 'Are you the leader of this orchestra?' Starnberg answered that he was. 'Then give me a list if you have one, and if you don't have one, start writing one.'

There was no decision to make. Starnberg opened his case and took out an old programme on which was printed a list of the players, crossing off the names of the two violinists who were killed trying to escape, and those of the three men who had leapt from the train before it was captured. Kondal took it, and walked out.

Another morning went by. Starnberg did not bother to watch it go, but felt it pass with eyes closed, ignoring the small promptings that told him to get up and go to the window, to look out between the bars and listen at every small sound, to smell the dew and grass, and see if the cat were still there. They had heard nothing, and everyone stayed locked in yesterday's mind. They had ceased to hope. They did not think as yet that they were going to be

137

killed however; it was merely that hope had put a strain on them, and they found it less enervating to live from day to day, in a vacuum, neither in hope nor in despair, in the numbed realization that they were prisoners.

Armgardson was sullen, Evart talkative, Starnberg weary. Shells never ceased booming and smashing into the hills through each minute of the black, rain-sodden night. Clouds came and went, sweeping cold rain against every hidden inch of ground. Doors were opened and closed almost without being noticed. In the card game an inflated currency of cigarettes in danger of disintegrating through too much handling were divided out and smoked.

No one slept in the afternoon, having lost confidence in the curative powers of repose. Those lying down kept their eyes open. Some had coats pulled over them because it was no longer warm, while others sat with shirt sleeves rolled up, not noticing the cold. Over the card table cigarette smoke rose with the noise and rattle of keen argument; the game went on beneath lighted lamps because the black and red symbols could no longer be clearly seen. Starnberg heard the page of a book being turned and, having noticed that, was aware of the guns again, forced out of a blank reverie by their incoherent language. He saw Armgardson back at the window, his head pressed against the bars, his eyes watching dull clouds over the hills. From the total conversation he caught the voice of someone arguing on the best way to cook an omelette, and other voices discussing female morals. The game must have risen to a climax, because the players were quiet and intent, watching their last cards.

Evart said he could see no more hope in Starnberg's face, and Starnberg replied that perhaps his face was too tired to show it, but that it was there just the same. This reply seemed to satisfy Evart and he did not speak for a while. Starnberg noticed that many sat with legs outstretched at right angles to their bodies, which seemed to him such a sign of hopelessness that he tried to avoid falling into it himself, an effort that made him smile because he knew he was just as much inclined to it as they were. Evart sat in that position, but his shade of hopelessness was relieved by him smoking a cigarette, and by the smile he occasionally gave. 'Judging from the sound of the guns it seems that the General's going to start another attack,' he said to Starnberg.

'Perhaps. I can't tell. I've never been near a war before.'

'Neither have I. It's just a guess.' The dampness made him shiver, so he buttoned his coat. 'But I wish we were away from the sound of them. I'm always ready to fall asleep by nine o'clock in the evening, as though I'd done a full day's work, but it's really because the guns have been wearing my energy away all day long, even though I don't seem to notice them most of the time.'

'You can get used to it after a while,' Starnberg said. 'Like music on the radio that you don't want to hear; your senses simply ignore it.'

'The sound of guns is different. My senses don't want to hear it, obviously, but it goes right to their base and undermines them; guns have so much meaning that they can't be ignored. Not even partly. Every explosion has some meaning, probably a different one each time. To some of them I want to stand up and shout: "Stop!" to others I'm quite content to listen without any feelings; and then there are times when I say, "Good, good, that was wonderful. Keep on firing, blowing-up, smashing," after each shell bursts.'

'What if every shell were coming towards you?' Starnberg pertinently suggested.

'I'd hope,' he grinned, 'as I'd never hoped before. At least I'd soon know whether my hopes were to be fulfilled or not.'

'Still, I'd rather be out of it altogether.'

'So would I. Guns breed bad thoughts. I often wonder

what it'll be like when they aren't continually firing like this. It'll be strange to hear no more guns. And that makes me think of all the different sorts of sounds I've ever heard, and wonder what the last sound will be when I die. Will it be a pleasant sound? Or a cruel sound? It's amusing to speculate.'

Starnberg said: 'I'd like to know why the officer came in for our names yesterday. Such official action frightens me.'

'It was nothing. He should have made the list as soon as we were captured, but didn't remember until yesterday.'

'Why did you refuse to give it to him? That was the most unnerving thing about it. I thought you were trying to kill yourself.'

'I didn't like his manner,' Evart replied, altering the position of his legs so that he could draw them more comfortably towards his stomach. 'The sight of him put me into a rage. These people who've captured us, they're like the evil spilling out of a dream. That's a very bad cliché, but clichés are sometimes so true that you've got to use them. The Gorsheks are overrunning the earth with their barbarisms, and I've come to realize in the last few days that they're like something hidden in my own nature, something that's quiescent though, that I hardly need to fight. If it stopped being quiescent I should fight it, because if I didn't I'd be one of these people. I'd fight it just as I suppose we should have fought the Gorsheks ever since they came against us – or we went against them.'

'But they're already being fought,' Starnberg reminded him.

'Not by us,' he retorted.

'We're doing the best we can by waiting here patiently. And in any case we can't fight them. We couldn't fight even if we were free. We aren't soldiers.'

'I know,' Evart said harshly. 'We're in an impossible situation whichever way you look at it. Even on the other side of those mountains we couldn't fight, no matter how

140

much we thought it necessary. The fighting must be left to others, and if those others win it'll be they who'll parcel our freedom out to us. We can only hope that they'll give us a bit more than we'd get if we were conquered by these people. We're at a point when we hope that the lesser evil will prevail, which is the most any artist or entertainer can hope for when a war starts. The only problem now is that it's so difficult to know which is the lesser evil. Our government treats us so badly that we immediately try to believe that the other side would treat us better. Even now, who knows that the Gorsheks wouldn't? They may kill prisoners, but their peculiar brand of art flourishes. The only reason why we have to fight them is that their art is so different from ours that we could never practise it. Fortunately we have our own ideas for which we'd like to fight, but we've neither the strength nor the nature to fight for them. The truth of it is that we don't even want to fight for those freedoms that we must have, but want the others, the generals and soldiers, to fight and preserve them for us, which is asking too much. If they lost a war and those freedoms were taken from us, we'd hold them to blame; if they won a war and denied us those freedoms, we'd still blame them. So what can we do?' Others were listening, but Evart was beyond noticing: 'Not much, perhaps,' he answered himself. 'The one and only visionary course open to us is to fight our government even harder than the Gorsheks. Revolutionaries in mind, we should become revolutionaries in action. Fight anyone who would make slaves of us. Act now, and turn to the edifice of our own government.' A fire had been lit within his brain: 'Why have I only seen it at this moment, when it's too late?'

'Maybe it isn't too late?' Starnberg reminded him.

Evart could not go back to his reading. He wondered, like everyone else in varying degrees of consciousness, what was going to happen. He had never known such a time as this, in which the future absolutely did not exist. Time went unbearably slower now that they were forced to live by the hour, and he supposed that such an experience – if lived through – turned a man into a philosopher, forcing him to contemplate a future that he could neither see nor understand nor materially hope to expect, thus filling him with endless speculation. A man who is uncertain whether or not he is condemned to die keeps his sanity in this way: by organizing the thoughts that are with him while he waits to find out. Evart imagined that this lethargy would leave them if the General were to come in and demand to hear another symphony. But there was no sign of him doing so. The usual noises surrounded his house across the road: occasional traffic, shouts, and the coming and going of soldiers. Evart pictured it so well that the barn doors might have been open. Equally, he came to see his own thoughts so clearly that the cover might just as well have been pulled back from his mind.

And the final double-barrelled question persisted: What is going to happen, and when will it happen?

No one sat at the card table. Hardly anyone talked. Very few even sat up. They either read or slept. It was growing dark already, and Evart supposed someone would get up and light the lamps. But whatever happens, he thought, I feel strongly that we'll know quite soon the way things are going to turn out.

Only one man was not lying down. He stood at the window looking through the bars. The shadows were so heavy that no one could tell who it was.

Evart stood up to light the lamps.

12

Facing the veranda of the General's house lay a ruined street, straight, black, forbidding, crossed by shadows and starving cats. Dark shapes of peeled and splintered tree trunks joined one wall to another, as if both sides of the street had thought to shake hands at the moment of catastrophe. Cellars, open to the night stars and filled with rubble, were beyond the range of the lamp shining down on the General's table, though the street was not unconnected with similar black highways in his mind.

He stretched out his legs beneath the wickerwork table and poured another drink. It was a warm moonless night with many stars, and a tree from the garden spread a good proportion of its branches over the steps and rail of the veranda. He drained the glass, felt the burning colourless liquid descend into his stomach, then poured himself another. A miracle, he thought, that this house and that tree weren't even scorched or scarred by shells, yet a further miracle won't come to save me from the dilemma of the orchestra. He had hopes for an enemy counterattack, a dangerous and exciting situation that would bury the problem, but even so, High Command would never forget them, would demand again – after he had contained and smashed the attack – to know why they had not been killed. He saw clearly that there was no solution outside of himself, and he was left alone fighting an impossible monster in the dark that would neither kill him nor let him live.

He struck a match to light his cigarette. The unsteady light flared for a second, gained on the weak electricity, showed the grey colour of his uniform, the gleam of his buttons and the shine of his gaiters. He blew it out and laid the charred remains in the ashtray, leaving his face in electric-light shadow. The guns seemed to be bombarding his conscience into submission, but their flashes also illuminated the condition of his mind after surrender, a sight which forced him to prolong the battle. By doing so he discovered that the mind resembled a box of magician's tricks: you either learned to control the various aspects of them, by juggling, dodging, legerdemain, a certain amount of knowledge; or they came to manipulate you, by clockhands, hammerblows and baited traps. In the latter event, you lost your reason.

It would be easier to kill myself, he thought grimly, then I'd be rid of it all; though why do I think of killing myself when I won't risk my life trying to save them? Because I wouldn't succeed, and there's more nobility in suicide. It was a slick answer, and he distrusted it, which caused more pain, and his argument evolved to the self-centred realistic fact that he wouldn't sacrifice his life to save them because he considered himself more valuable to the Gorshek nation than a symphony orchestra was to the world.

He clapped his hands, and a blade of light sloped across the veranda, made a frame that the servant stepped into.

'Another bottle.'

'Yes, your excellency.'

A third signal had been flashed to his office from High Command, demanding immediate answer to its enquiries about the orchestra. When he thought of it, and saw again the pencilled block capitals that were as characterless as the signaller's fingers and mind that had written them, he shivered at what his long delay of the executions could mean. The frame of light remained on the veranda, and the servant came through it, placed a bottle on the table, and waited for another order.

'I can pour it myself.'

The figure retreated, taking his frame of light behind him. The pleasant sound of drink filling the glass drove all thoughts from the General's mind, but no sooner did the drink touch his lips than they returned, forcing him to ask: Why don't I want to kill them? – a question that he could not for the moment answer, that his mind veered away from as if it were a bar of glowing iron. Then why must I kill them? Because High Command want me to. He tried to ponder several minutes before his answer, but it came too precisely and automatically for him to gain any advantage from such tactics. Is there no way I can save them? This time the question came after the answer, with the same result. In the eyes of High Command there's no reason to keep them alive – all the arguments passed through his mind once more – because they have no value, can do nothing to help the war, will not lift the officers' morale if allowed to give concerts in the barn, will prove of no use if put to repairing roads or digging fields, for we have all the labour we need, according to High Command.

He stood up and, leaving his hat behind, descended the veranda steps, perhaps, he thought while crossing the road, with the idea of escaping Kondal who was due at the house in an hour to remind him of his decision to massacre the orchestra that night. He checked himself from crying out. How can I live after killing them? I'll be merely obeying an order, but my conscience won't take care of me, because I think that I can somehow still save them. I can't save them. If I don't kill them, others will, so why should I uselessly sacrifice myself? The voice of reason, the voice of madness, the voice of duty and the voice of conscience tell me to do different things. I have only one voice, that can speak or say nothing – but which must make up its mind.

Unknowingly he walked into the ruined street, climbing over trees, and stepping on blistered house-sides that had fallen intact across the paving. He could not see where he was going, put out his hands that touched doors and doorknobs wedged down by branches, felt cool leaves and fungus that had sprouted from inhospitable nests since the bombardment had smashed most of the village to pieces, caught hold of soaked cloths and wallpaper and hands. No, he thought, drawing back, my mind has been made up for me. High Command have sent three signals, and my orders are on them. Rats, losing their bravery for a moment, scampered away at his approach, their red eyes gleaming from distant beams as he went by. Can't I let them escape? I could never explain it. Besides, none of them would finally get back to their own land. They wouldn't cross the front line. They'd be caught one by one and tortured to death by my soldiers. Yet there'd be a possibility of their getting back if I gave them guns and released them. Would they accept guns from me? Can I plead for them with High Command? No, my campaigns have been too successful. They'd purposely humiliate me by refusing. Perhaps they don't want to win the war as quickly as I look like doing. It might make good propaganda to humiliate me, and in any case they think I'm becoming too popular, too power-ful. They don't trust me as much as they once did. They think I may try a rebellion.

He was lost, having turned off the main street, treading over broken glass in complete darkness. Lifting his hand he drew it close to his eyes, but was unable to see it, as if he had gone blind. He wandered about in the ruins, feeling his way forward with feet and hands, scratching himself on thorns and splinters.

What can I do?

Nothing.

'What can I do?' he called out aloud.

'Nothing,' a real voice answered, springing from his own mouth. A heap of glass and rubble shifted beneath his feet, causing him to slip, to crash down sideways as the glass subsided into another floor. A beam scraped along his leg, and he went on falling, his nostrils pierced by smells of rot and dampness. A sharp pain opened his arm, feeling as if the rot and dampness had made a javelin point and cut into him. It became painless. He landed in the cellar on the same arm, bringing down wood and plaster, half bricks, soil and bones. The noise of his fall filled the whole world, but he lay there for what seemed a long time, one hand feeling around to make sure he was on solid ground.

A rat stirred, left what it had been feeding on, came towards him, stopped – then veered away, squeaking with disappointment, as if aware that the General had already unhooked his revolver and pointed it at its eyes. Complete freedom, he thought, would be unutterable pain. I've the opportunity of making a momentous decision, which is as much freedom as I can bear. He felt as if all his blood were flowing away from him. His eyes closed, and beyond a barrier of sleep, in the greater, more comfortable darkness he saw the portrait of the dead Gorshek hero in all its detail and colour hanging by the door in his office. Of course, he thought, how obvious, how strange that I haven't noticed it before. I knew the face was familiar. It's Kondal! The ideal officer who will take my place: ruthless, obedient, happy. A door opened and light squared itself over the rubble. Kondal stood in it.

The General did not want to see anything, tried to ignore the lit-up doorway, as if unwilling to believe in what he witnessed from the black pit of his deathlike sleep. The figure moved, but he did not know whether it had lifted an arm or turned its head, only that it had moved, because he noticed part of the shadow change direction and then stay still. He wants to tell me that the orchestra are in the barn, waiting to be murdered. Kondal shuffled his feet, trying in a respectful way to attract attention.

'Well?' the General said, 'what do you want?' They've come to tear me to pieces. Why had Kondal grown so tall?

'Your excellency, the prisoners. You told me to remind

you.' He stepped forward from the doorway and stood closer: 'Are the prisoners to be shot?'

The General shook away blood that had crept over his eyes. 'Yes, shoot them,' he roared. 'Do you hear me? Shoot them.' He waved his arm and the filled bottle must have fallen on to him because his sleeve was wet. Some of the liquid dropped on to his knees, oozed through to his skin until it became thick like mud. 'Shoot them now,' he shouted. 'This minute. Do you hear me?' His distorted features looked into the officer's face, which moved away and vanished. He struck at it with his clenched fist.

The regular monotone of marching feet penetrated his ears and, realizing that the noise was coming closer, he began to listen intently, gradually detecting other sounds encased around them. The marching paved a way through everything else, until soldiers' boots trod the ground in unison not far away. They must have halted before the barn, in response to Kondal's angry voice, and he continued to listen with detached interest. Such lack of emotion surprised him, though he felt that it was pleasant, and did not care to disturb it. Feet mingled eagerly with the touch of hands on rifles as Kondal's order was obeyed, and the General noticed drops of rain falling, and a cold wind drifting into his cellar so that he shivered, unable to move, hands gripping scattered bricks and rubble. He became alarmed that his mind should be drained of thoughts at such a moment, but he possessed no power to control it, and could only go on listening. Someone was opening the barn door: it scraped along the ground and the hinges screeched. Kondal's loud words could not be distinguished, for he was too far away, and then his speech was suddenly overcome by voices of panic and defiance. The General hoped that the shouting would stop, but it went on like a remorseless growth. A clock chimed, beat out ten strokes and at every stroke his fingers tightened and loosened their hold, cutting themselves on broken slate and laths. He tried to move his eyes out of their fixed stare. Why do they make it so hard for themselves? he asked. Single shouts were welded together by roars of confusion and alarm, and the soldiers also began shouting. What can I do? he wondered, but relapsed immediately into his negative state, the final womb-like refuge of a defeated commander. The running of one man's feet was followed by an order telling him to stop, and his progress was drowned by rising voices. In a trough of sound the first shot was fired, its clatter echoing through the village, and before it died away volleys began rolling against the barn like onslaughts of thunder. Flashes penetrated the General's staring eyes, and bursts of firing stung his emptied mind until thoughts began to come back. Vibrations ingrained themselves through the ground beneath him, bullets dancing around him like feet in madness, engulfing him like an angry cloak, drumming away to the four ends of the earth. He shivered and rubbed raindrops from his wrist: then a cry from the orchestra came louder than all the rest and made him hope that it was the last one, but it went on for a long time, in a slow diabolical attenuation that forced him to sit with hands over his ears, keep his eyes closed, and wish that the roll of fire would cease, that the cries it caused would bury themselves under the earth.

He awoke. A drunken man could be heard wailing from another street. Where am I? Pain had slipped a burning noose over the left side of his body and was drawing it tighter, the gravitational centre marked by a bloodsoaked forearm. He stood up and wandered around slowly, until he came against the staircase-wall of the cellar and felt a cold wind funnelled strongly through some open trapdoor above. Following each stone right-angle down with his fingers, he swept away slippery glass and cement, an action that steadied his reawakened mind and helped him to ascend to the ruins and open air.

The area was lit up almost continually with shellfire, and by the light of its flashes he recognized the direction from which he had strayed, and subsequent salvoes pinpointed his track towards the house. Stars became visible again, shining through isolated windows, showing the occasional tall, solitary wall of a house still standing, like a makeshift crutch holding up the sky. Clutching his arm he crossed the road and stumbled against the veranda steps. A sudden throb of pain made him gasp, was so intense that the thought that it would never go pushed him to the verge of a bleak unexplored landscape of the mind where dignity did not exist: but he held back silently, until the pang settled. He regained the table, filled his glass and drank the liquid, refilling again and again, as if it were loot, and the enemy about to retake it from his fingers.

An hour later, his arm bandaged, he met Kondal on the road before the house. 'You're late,' the General forestalled him. 'You were coming to ask me about the orchestra, as I told you to, but you should have been here an hour ago.'

Kondal nodded. 'Yes, your excellency, but there was a mutiny. A company of the 198th Battalion refused to go up to the pass. But they've gone now.'

Efficient, the General thought. Ruthless. So that's what it was. 'Do you have any confidence,' he asked Kondal, 'in the success of my plans?' He waited for an affirmative in the correct tone of voice, then went on, speaking in the official textbook language in which Kondal delighted: 'I suppose you've been puzzled during the last few days as to why I haven't yet killed the prisoners in the barn? Well, as you should know by now, I have a reason for everything, and my reasons for not killing the orchestra, even though High Command have ordered me to do so, are of supreme importance, for they have to do with next spring's offensive. It's been my intention for some days to send a group of spies over the mountains to report on movements at the pass. There'll be about a hundred of them, and their orders will be to keep together when they reach the plain, so that the enemy will find it beyond the powers of their military police to track them down and will be forced to institute a minor campaign in order to do so, and when my hundred spies are surrounded they'll be able to report to me by radio what units are sent against them before they are wiped out. I want to see to what extent the enemy have been reinforced on that part of the front and see if the report of massive additions to their forces was correct. Now, Kondal, listen: I arranged a few days ago for one man to be accidentally captured with papers in his pocket stating the time and route of the spies' intended crossing. The enemy will think I'm bluffing, but in any case will guard the place, normally so high that it's merely patrolled. To their surprise they'll see a group approaching who'll call out that they are their own people, members of an orchestra recently captured by us, the Gorsheks. They'll be shot down of course. Two days later my real spies will go over, when they aren't expected, and when the area is again only patrolled.'

Kondal's eyes could not be seen in the darkness, but he said, with a tone of amusement: 'I understand your excellency very well. The orchestra will have quite a surprise.'

'And so that they'll think I'm really giving them the chance to escape, and don't suspect my trick,' the General went on, perceiving that Kondal thought a great deal of his plan, 'I'm going to supply them with rifles, ammunition and food, and I'll give them a map, with directions on how to reach the spot where the enemy are waiting for them in the mountains.'

Kondal nodded once more, quickly realizing what he must do. 'I'll take some soldiers immediately to collect guns and supplies then, your excellency.' He walked towards the guards' quarters.

High Command will be more difficult to bluff, the

General thought. There's nothing else to argue about. I've taken the first step. He stood for a few minutes pondering in the darkness, then made his way across open ground to the barn.

Two soldiers at the door entered with him. Most of the orchestra were asleep: he had sent them no fuel for the lamps during the last two days, and they were strange people who could not sit and talk for hours in complete darkness like his soldiers. They disliked the dark in which they could not see each other, and had to see a face before they could read a man's thoughts. Did Kondal read mine? he wondered.

Evart stood up, glad to have been held back from a sleep that showed no sign of coming. On seeing the General he knew that some decision had been made at last. Why is it to happen at night, and not in the morning? he wondered. It's less cruel to kill someone at dawn, when they have more courage. The General unfolded a map as he walked towards him.

'I've drawn a line that you and your orchestra are to follow, and with luck you should be over the mountains in two days,' he said with a smile, though finding no happiness or elation in what he was doing. He asked himself again why he was setting them free, but could not answer, only aware that there was no alternative but this, and that even when they had gone he could not regret what he was now about to do. The only guiding thought that came to him was: it's a fanatical action – and because the result of following this thought to its logical conclusion would be not to act at all he resumed his instructions to Evart, the leader of the orchestra who only now began to realize that the General meant what he said.

Kondal and several soldiers came in with rifles and supplies, and the orchestra, though also aware of what was happening, stood around silently.

'Here are rifles, ammunition and food,' the General said

152

in a low voice. 'Look at this map' – Evart read it over his shoulder – 'Cross the railway line and walk north. Pinpoint yourselves on 504, then trek at right angles to the Northern Star and go over the road left of the wood. When you reach the river follow it up-course and don't cross until you come to a ford that leaves you clear of the trees. Negotiate it there, and follow the rough track leading between 1097 and 644. Keep together and walk silently. Your route is the boundary of two brigades and not well guarded. I shall order the flanking screens of each to draw into their centres, and command the guns to keep silent on that sector. The only danger will be when you come to the skirmish-lines and outposts of your own soldiers: but that is up to you.'

'The only thing is,' Evart said, 'that we don't need rifles.'

The General had expected this condition to be made. 'I disagree. It's more than likely that you'll need them. But if you refuse to take them, I shan't give you either the food or the map.'

'Our instruments?'

'Will stay in the barn.'

Kondal dismissed the soldiers and gave the first rifle and belt of pouches to Armgardson, who slung them across his shoulder and began filling his pockets with bread. He then put on his overcoat inside out and fastened it at the waist with a piece of rope. Schelter, Viccadi, Starnberg and Bender also accepted guns, until the whole orchestra was armed, most of them willingly, some distastefully, and a few indifferent. Armgardson took a great deal of interest in his gun, examined it from sling to muzzle with the air of an expert smith, ran his hand along the woodwork, lifted the sights and aligned them with the far corner of the barn, and loaded the magazine with as many bullets as it would take. 'At last,' he exclaimed between his teeth. 'At last.'

Finally, Evart took a gun. 'You win,' he said to the General.

'Every battle but the last,' he answered.

'Why don't you come with us?' Starnberg asked.

The General unconsciously whistled a few bars of some patriotic tune, until Starnberg was called away; he then watched them file out in silence. Kondal stood grinning by his side.

They were some distance from the barn, treading over soft damp soil, walking west and keeping the dark shape of the village to the right. A cold wind blew against them from the mountains, as if to bar their passage in that direction. Evart sensed that a deep autumn had finally descended on the enormous sodden land, for even in darkness and danger it nostalgically brought back other autumns in other faraway countries – the same smell, soily dampness and premature rot infested the air so heavily that he found himself enmeshed in a host of memories it recalled.

He halted, motioned the others to keep together, and in the silence the sound of a single shot reached them from the barn. He paused for a moment, as if to make sure he had heard it, and as if to confirm the first report for him another shot sounded dully in the air. He then went on, carrying the unaccustomed burden of a loaded rifle, and another familiar burden to which he could as yet give no name.

13

After several hours in a windswept siding the crowded open railway trucks were coupled to a train and began rolling slowly westwards. Groans of relief rose from the starving half naked prisoners, accompanied by a dull jangle of chains as they sat up to see where they were going. The train traversed flat ground between steel rolling mills and munition works, skirting rusty grass-choked tramlines, and turned between low-roofed housing estates. Each suburban living-unit that had once housed a hundred thousand people was dominated by a tall administrative building from which the national flags had been removed. Windows were cross-planked and creosoted, doorways stuffed with bracken and paper, ready to burn and gut every building for as far as the eye could see, should there not be enough explosives to destroy them utterly. Groups of dull-eyed people stood mutely by the line watching the long train pass.

Soon, the General thought, as the last ragged edges of the city gave way to green plain, all this machinery will be evacuated, and these buildings finished-off; they'll pack a hundred million people into a vast perimeter at the end of the continent and hope to hold out from there, to spring forth again like tigers at a later date. Since the trial his sector of the front had received the full impact of a counter-offensive, and had collapsed. The network of his complex preparations had perished in the clumsy brain to which they had been passed on at the time of his arrest. The opposing armies shattered his defence works at the very point from which he had thought to break out: earth had fallen on to and smothered his assembling Knife Battalions

155

in their underground waiting stations; water had rushed in on concealed provisions; fire had found the secret recesses of his explosive stores. It was a vile winter blow economically made by an enemy who possessed an unparalleled cupidity for the hours and days of each life in its possession. The wound in the mountain range left the régime divided in opinion, one party wanting to march all available armies against the scorched and bleeding gap, the other to retreat to a safe line of mountains and great rivers in the north and west.

The guards ordered him to get down into the truck, and though he mechanically obeyed, they followed the order with several stones, some of which struck him on the face and forearm, causing him to jerk both places back against the board. No longer able to look at the landscape, he lifted his head to the grey sky where heavy rolls of mist deepened, and prophesied rain. As he sat on the hard uncomfortable floor of the truck, crowded in by other exiles, the wearisome days of his trial came back to him. The officers who had heard the symphony reported the postponement of the massacre to High Command, and testified to the orchestra's disappearance, saying that they only attended the concert because he, exerting pressure of rank, had forced them to do so. Then came the affair of Kondal's death. They tried to prove he was insane, saying that he had shot Kondal twice in the face without knowing what he was doing, that he had committed the deed on impulse, at a time when he was suffering from the reaction of overwork from his last offensive. But he had deliberately killed Kondal, and no amount of word-twisting could turn it into an accident. Before the trial they did their best to drive him insane so as to prove their point, but his mind had achieved a certain flexibility from his struggle with the problem of the orchestra, so they did not succeed. He coolly assured them of his sanity right to the end.

The air was bleak, damp and biting; he shivered in the

rawness of the morning. The other prisoners sat with no expression in their eyes, with sackcloth uniforms pulled around them, with chilled faces, their only pastime being to scratch the chafed flesh beneath heavy manacles. The guards in their greatcoats, furs and caps, stood at each corner of the truck, pointing machine guns at the prisoners, shouting abruptly to each other, now and again commenting on certain familiar landmarks that the train passed. And so the evidence was built up against me, and the charge list was so long that I didn't understand what they were talking about in the last days of the trial. He laughed to himself: they tried to humiliate me by padding the evidence with crude insults, but after the orchestra was set free and Kondal dead I was impervious to anything for a long time. 'Are you guilty?' they had demanded. 'No,' I told them. And they were surprised, having expected me to say I was guilty and to tell them why, and I was happy at seeing how surprised they were. It was the first time I had been happy for a long time, and everyone was puzzled except me. But they should ask me again, now, whether or not I believe I am guilty. It's only after the trial that a prisoner is able to answer such a question – since everything has to be taken into consideration.

The train jolted to a stop and lay in the shadow of some trees. No sooner had the guards begun to discuss why it had done so, when a sudden move took them forward again. The wind was changing direction, and engine smoke now coiled directly above the truck. He shifted his body from the discomfort of sitting penned in one position, but nudged the man next to him, who grunted so menacingly that he went back to where he had been before and sat glumly looking at the shaved back of another man's head. Reminded of his own flesh he braced both face and forearm against the pain where the recent stones had struck. Deprived of sufficient food he had become more sensitive to pain – and everything else. To preserve his life he felt himself an island, an isolated man out of contact with his fellow beasts – though at large on a sea of them – as much an island as the small areas of shifting pain to which he was now and again subjected, and which he knew – in strong enough terms – that he would always endure. No wonder. My crime was enormous in their view, he thought, but for me I'll never admit to a crime at all. Two forms of punishment were given for 'direct wickedness against the common cause of the régime'. The most humane of the two, the infinitely preferable, was to be taken out and shot; the most severe, to which he had been sentenced, was exile until death. Because of this there were times when he not unnaturally regretted the sudden end of his career, when he asked himself why he had ever seen the orchestra, cursed himself for a sentimental fool, and wished he had sent them to High Command headquarters as soon as Kondal brought them back from the battlefield. Even that wouldn't have been necessary if the train hadn't run through our attack; it should have been stopped before it reached the lines. He remembered the endless investigations carried out for the trial, in which it was discovered that the train drivers that brought the orchestra through had been hopelessly drunk.

While ruminating on his fate a familiar sound seemed to be hovering just outside the noise of moving wheels, and he wanted to stand up so as to bring it within range, but he knew that the guards would order him down, even if he would be able to support the weight of his chains. From his sitting position he could hear it only as an indistinct murmur playing above the struggles of the long shunting train. He dwelt, as he had done a thousand times already, on the stupidity of the horseman who had leapt into the orchestra's train and stopped it by threatening the drivers with his pistol. Why hadn't he left it to crash instead of risking his worthless life to stop it? But, he told himself, we've no power to alter the circumstances that are unknowingly shaping our lives. We can only wait, in our happy oblivion, or hopeful suffering, for the results of these unknown movements to affect us. The biggest fools of all were the members of the orchestra. They didn't even think of pulling the communication cord to stop the train and make their escape in the confusion. They must surely have seen what was happening: that the train was running into a battle.

A rumbling came again above the train's progress, like a faint throb of pain in a faraway part of the wounded sky. The guards heard it too, looked at each other, and wondered what it could be. Then the train stopped again, so that its noise no longer interfered with the General's sense of hearing.

Despite the endless spaces of the world's continents – seen for the first time as something more than matchless obstacles to the movement of troops – he viewed the whole world suddenly as a tiny area of the brain, an atom making up the total consciousness of any man. And life, he thought, is like a prison cell we are slung into by our birth – a limited room we are penned in and lifted from when we die. Who sentenced us to such a life? We never even had an opportunity of shouting and raving at the Judge: 'I didn't do it, Your Honour. I'm innocent! I'm innocent!' But we have to live out our sentence just the same, grow to like it in fact so that faced with the real freedom of death we become afraid and cower back against the wall.

A continual murmur of guns came from the north, from the direction of the wind. He had not heard the sound for a long time, and listened to it intently, deciding that they were of a heavy type firing from forty miles away. Even though the train had stopped he could only hear them at certain times, as if their sounds lifted and dropped on their way over the land. There are many messages in the sound of guns, he smiled to himself. They mean hope, and death, and destruction, and a new way of life perhaps, and the primitive wars of human beings for conquest and freedom. Noise – the secret messages preceding change, and whose cipher is broken by history.

The train lurched forward, and he only heard the guns now in his imagination. A fine drizzle came down. Hills lay before them and the train went still slower as it toiled up a gradient. From time to time he heard the faintest tremble of bombardment: the noise kept losing itself, but came back to him when he listened carefully. Rain pitted against his cheeks; he moved the spade away from his feet, and drew the thin uniform tightly around him in an effort to keep out the dampness and cold.